FAMILIES and SURVIVORS

by Alice Adams

PENGUIN BOOKS

PENGUIN BOOKS

Viking Penguin Inc., 40 West 23rd Street,
New York, New York 10010, U.S.A.
Penguin Books Ltd, Harmondsworth,
Middlesex, England
Penguin Books Australia Ltd, Ringwood,
Victoria, Australia
Penguin Books Canada Limited, 2801 John Street,
Markham, Ontario, Canada L3R 1B4
Penguin Books (N.Z.) Ltd, 182–190 Wairau Road,
Auckland 10, New Zealand

First published in the United States of America by
Alfred A. Knopf, Inc., 1974
First published in Canada by
Random House of Canada Limited 1974
Published by Viking Penguin Inc. 1984

LIBRARY OF CONGRESS CATALOGING IN PUBLICATION DATA
Adams, Alice, 1926–
Families and survivors.
(Penguin contemporary American fiction series)
Reprint. Originally published: New York: Knopf, 1975.
I. Title. II. Series.
[PS3551.D324F3 1984] 813'.54 84-6447
ISBN 0 14 00.7375 2

Printed in the United States of America

Set in Linotype Janson

TO:

Lucie Jessner

Peter Adams Linenthal

AND

Robert K. McNie

WITH LOVE

Families and Survivors

One / 1941

On the wide edge of a large kidney-shaped swimming pool sit two naked fourteen-year-old girls, Louisa Calloway and Kate Flickinger. It is a heavily hot and humid night in May, in Virginia. Unlit lamps are hung all about the pool; in the dark the water glistens, barely moving, luminous. Around the pool are flowering shrubs, all blurs of white dim blooms, and the air smells indistinctly sweet.

From the house, some distance away from the pool, come the sounds of an adult party at its peak, a full continuous roar in which separate voices are absorbed. Later the noise will become discordant, broken by loud dissonant shouts, a few feminine shrieks.

Louisa Calloway (it is her tobacco-rich father's pool) stretches her legs out before her, then brings them back, bent, to her right side. She puts her arms behind her, hands flat, and arches her chest. Tiny nipples stand out, and long brown hair swings back. "Sex appeal!" she whispers loudly.

Then she bursts out laughing.

Kate laughs, too—in fact they are both almost hysterical; laughter pushes upward in their throats.

Kate lies down on her side, supporting herself on an elbow; she crosses her feet at the ankles and sticks out her chest. She has hard conical breasts. "Sex appeal!"

It is the funniest thing they have ever done, and they invent posture after posture. They choke on their own wit: the sight of their posed flesh makes them hilarious. Lana Turner! Ann Sheridan! Hedy! "Sex appeal!"

Finally, and funniest of all, from an extreme posture—she is almost doing a split—Louisa topples into the pool, and laughing Kate tumbles in, too, and still laughing they swim about, in the warm moonless dark.

Then Kate says, "Damn! What time do you think it is?"

"I'll see." Louisa swims over to where she left her watch, and peers at the dial. "Ten-thirty."

"Damn! I haven't done my history. The test tomorrow."

They both climb out; they dry themselves on large towels that have been draped over the picnic chairs; they sort out their clothes from the pile on the table: bras, shirts, pants, shorts, sneakers.

"I suppose you know it all?" says Kate.

"Not really."

"You'll get an A anyway."

They are walking on a path that winds between huge and ancient boxwood. They pass the stable that houses Jack Calloway's two mares (Louisa hates to ride) and they come to a large and very manicured gravel parking area. Kate has left her bike beside the Calloway Cadillac. She picks it up and gets on.

"Well, see you tomorrow."

Kate bikes off on the country clay road to her house, a

half-mile away, and Louisa opens the back door, entering through the kitchen. Since the party was "informal," the maids have left, but the kitchen is stacked with dishes for their arrival in the morning. Louisa tiptoes (this is unnecessary) upstairs to her room, where, seated at her desk in the lamplight, she writes a poem. Then she draws a tiny illustration. She has done this every night for the past seven months.

Their friendship, Louisa's and Kate's, began the preceding fall.

"Some Yankees have moved into the old Hemenway place," Jack Calloway announces one day at lunch to his wife and daughter. "From Chicago, named Flickinger." Jack has blue-black Irish hair, blue eyes of steel.

"I believe I heard that rumor at the Altar Guild," says mild Caroline, his wife, whose coloring is indistinct, she is all pale shades of brown.

"There's a new girl—" Louisa begins, but she is silenced by her father, who was about to speak.

"Please don't interrupt," he says, not looking at his daughter. "Near neighbors—do you think we should pay them a call?" This last is ironic; for irony Jack uses an English accent.

"Do people still do that? Why not phone and ask them for a drink?"

Invited, the Flickingers come for a drink, bringing the daughter whom Louisa has seen in school.

Kate, the new girl, has beautiful dark red hair. She wears odd clothes—or, rather, markedly un-Southern clothes: pleated navy wool skirts, a polo coat. In that mild Southern climate (and because in the prewar period most of the families in town are relatively poor, except Louisa's family) the girls wear cotton dresses all winter, and when they do wear wool they choose (their mothers choose) pastels—pale pink or yellow sweaters, light blue spring coats. Louisa is interested in Kate. Although she is Southern (God knows, with those parents), Louisa feels herself an alien there.

"God, what a marvelous room!" says Kate, in her vehement (Yankee) way. "God, all those books! Oh, you've got Thomas Wolfe!"

"Yes." Louisa is in fact so enraptured with Thomas Wolfe that she affects diffidence. "Do you like him?"

"God, he's fantastic—absolutely marvelous. 'Lost, and by the wind grieved, ghost—' Doesn't that make your skin crawl?"

"He's very good," Louisa says judiciously, feeling the cool crawl of those words on her skin as she speaks.

None of the other girls in town have read Thomas Wolfe, and almost on that basis the two girls become friends.

As their parents do; the grownups drink a lot and exchange stories of European travel. Watchful Caroline decides that Jane Flickinger is not at all Jack's type: Jane is tall and dark, forthright, and Jack likes small, fluffy blondes. Caroline sighs: at last a safe friendship. (She is wrong.)

Kate and Louisa take walks in the woods that surround the town, through bright fall leaves, then over a light sprinkling of snow. "One winter in Illinois it was over six feet deep," Kate tells her friend. "Oh, really?" This is Louisa's standard response, but she is secretly impressed, and she passionately tries to imagine such a snow. In the spring they walk beside the swollen brown creek out to Morgan's Bend, where a hillside has burst into pink, an explosion of rhododendron, among the pines. "God, it's so beautiful!" Kate says.

Sometimes they talk about the other girls, who are

only interested in boys, and about the boys, who are stupid.

The most popular girl is Snubby MacDonald. She is small, with long blond curls.

"She's so obvious," says Kate. "Every time that Richard Trowbridge comes around."

"Richard Trowbridge is one of the stupidest boys in town," Louisa says. "I've always known that."

"I *know*. God, sometimes he calls me up."

"He *does*?"

"Oh, yes, wants to go to a movie or something. I always say I'm busy."

"Oh, really?" Having regained her calm, Louisa is still impressed; most girls would have told about phone calls from Richard, who may have been stupid (later, when Louisa is in love with him, she finds that he is not stupid at all) but who is very good-looking, blond, with a slow, assured walk—and his parents are almost as rich as Louisa's are.

Richard Trowbridge is a popular boy, but the most truly desirable boy, for whom best friends among the girls will confess a secret (and shared) yearning, is John Jeffreys. John is a darkly handsome, thin, elusive boy: a basketball star who gets good grades, who plays the piano at parties (sometimes, when he feels like it) and has a fantastic collection of records, but not the ordinary ones—Jimmy Lunceford, the Goodman Quintet, Bobby Hackett; Louis Armstrong (Louis who?). John likes Snubby MacDonald; sometimes he takes her to movies on Sunday afternoons, and the rumor is that they hold hands there. Snubby, like most Southern belles, is cautious rather than "fast."

A dance. In the school gymnasium, a building of corrugated tin, called the Tin Can. The air is heavy with the smell of gardenias, of the girls' flowery perfumes (Evening in

Paris is the favorite), and of everyone's anxious sweat. The room is too hot, but only the chaperones notice that. A record dance: from a mammoth jukebox (Jack Calloway's gift to the school, which is terribly embarrassing to his daughter—why couldn't he just have given some books?) comes the trumpet of Artie Shaw. "Oh, when they begin, begin the beguine—."

Louisa, in a pleated blue taffeta dress that her mother ordered from Best's, in New York, is dancing with Burton Knowles, a very short boy with a prodigious I.Q., as high as hers. He admires her mind. Louisa admires nothing about Burton, but she laughs wildly at everything he says, in the hope that someone will see and will think she is having a marvelous time and cut in on her. This is a technique that observably works, among Southern girls at dances.

Kate is with Richard Trowbridge, who grins foolishly with joy at his slight possession of her. Kate in scarlet: startling, *vividly* visible everywhere. (What Southern girl would wear red to a dance, expecially a red-haired girl?)

John Jeffreys is too tall for Snubby MacDonald; sometimes her upturned face hits his stomach with her chin. But she is very pretty, in pink tulle. Instead of gardenias, sophisticated John has sent a single white camellia, which she has pinned behind one ear. Snubby always gets a rush; she has never been known to finish a dance with the boy she started out with.

Suddenly something (Richard? This is dubious) makes Kate laugh. In the middle of a fancy jitterbug routine — Richard is a good dancer; she is excellent—she stops and clutches her throat, laughing her full deep laugh. Everyone looks, smiling at her, in her scarlet silk dress. She is incredibly attractive.

Someone has cut in on Snubby, and John is standing alone as she is danced away. He looks at Kate, his eyes smiling and curious, and Louisa sees his look.

"Most people are so superficial, don't you think?" Looking up to Louisa, jerking about on the dance floor, Burton sighs.

"Oh, really?"

The record ends. "In the Mood." Really good dancers know, as Kate and Richard know, which coda is the final one. They stop, Kate's laughter subsiding, and they stand together waiting for whatever comes next.

The Ink Spots: "Java Jive."

John Jeffreys taps Richard on the shoulder. "Break, please?"

But instead of begining to dance he takes Kate's hand and slowly leads her over to the bleachers at one side of the gym.

Sam Jackson breaks in on Louisa and Burton— another small bright boy, but at least he is funny. But she can't see John and Kate any more. Thinking of them Louisa feels a sort of tingling anticipation that is not entirely pleasant.

Glen Miller: "Sunrise Serenade."

That means that next will be "Moonlight Serenade," which by tradition means Last Dance: Escort, No Break. That is the rule at these dances.

Toward the end of "Sunrise," John leads Kate back to the floor. They seem to be having a serious conversation (about what?).

Snubby is dancing with Richard.

Burton cuts in on Louisa, to claim the last dance.

"Moonlight Serenade."

Kate and John go right on talking as they dance.

Looking at them, Snubby and Richard giggle. Within their hearing Richard says, "Do you think we should double-break on those people?"

"Oh, heavens, no—why bother?" Snubby has a tinkly little laugh, tinsel on a Christmas tree. She is also more intelligent than most people know. One afternoon, finding themselves alone in the principal's office, Louisa and Kate look up everyone's I.Q., and Snubby's is 135, which is hardly stupid. But she is Southern and smart enough to play it very dumb—a thing that Louisa refuses to do.

The dance is over; people clap.

Since the boys are too young to drive, various parents arrive in cars to take the couples home. There is Louisa's mother, Caroline, in her Cadillac, to take Louisa home, and Burton and Kate and Richard. Louisa gets in front with her mother, the other three in back.

"Well, darling, how was the dance?" Pained, languid Caroline—it is years before Louisa sees the anguish behind her mother's mask.

"Pretty much the same."

"Well, I'm sure you were the two prettiest girls there." (Can her mother mean this? Is she crazy—her too-tall wide-hipped daughter, whom mean whisperers name "built-for-birth"?)

"They were, Mrs. Calloway. I can assure you of that." Richard has very Southern manners, even including the faintest irony, which almost no one hears (and which, later in his life, is totally wasted in the C.I.A.).

Separately the boys are let off first—Kate is to spend the night at Louisa's house. What will she have to tell? Louisa listens in advance, imaginatively, as Kate tells her that she and John have fallen wildly in love, and they plan to elope to South Carolina, where you can get married at fourteen (or is it Maryland?); that he took her behind the bleachers and kissed her and put his hands on her breasts, and they will go off in the woods and lie down together, in a cave of honeysuckle.

"Well, girls, here we are," Caroline perfunctorily announces, in the driveway of their house.

Caroline and Jack have been having long after-dinner drinks on the side porch, in the warm leaf-stirred spring night. With Kenneth Mills—Dr. Mills—a family friend and also Jack's psychiatrist. Now Caroline and the girls go around to the side of the house, to where Jack and Kenneth still are. Kenneth is a lean, withdrawn man, generally considered handsome. He is married to Betsy, whom he often leaves at home. Jack likes Betsy, she is just his type — but in small doses. They all greet each other.

Jack has a refresher of a drink; Kenneth drinks more slowly. Jack is in a rare mood of great affection for both his wife and his daughter. He is a complicated, contradictory man; his ill-understood and violent emotions often seem hurled at his head from space, rather than arriving from within. "Well, my lovely ladies," he now asks, "how was the dance?"

"Fun," says Kate, and her dark eyes shine up at him.

"Louisa, you do look pretty," he says to his daughter. He has never said this before, and perhaps it is too late. "You liked the dance?"

Out of defensive habit she has to put him down. "If you like that sort of thing." And she shrugs.

Rejected, he is demon-driven to tease her. "Well, I'll bet that Snubby MacDonald enjoyed herself. When do I get to meet Snubby? She sounds like something more than okay."

And Kenneth echoes, "Yes, when do we meet Snubby?" He laughs quietly.

Louisa's heart freezes (as does Caroline's —ridiculously: a fifteen-year-old girl?). "I have a feeling that this wasn't exactly Snubby's favorite evening," says Louisa very snottily, with a curious look in Kenneth's direction. (A challenge, but to what?)

"Oh, why not? I wish I'd been there; I'd have cheered her up," Jack blusters desperately.

At that instant Caroline has a sudden (and accurate) and terrifying premonition: she sees that Louisa and Kenneth will fall in love; sometime, in a few years, Kenneth will make love to Louisa. Her heart turns colder. Yet how can she know this—how can she have this witch knowledge? Is it because she herself has a sort of "crush" on Kenneth? ("Crush," her word of disdain for her own emotions.) She is frozen, sitting there on her porch, with her husband and daughter and friends, in the warm summer night.

"I guess we'll go on up to bed," Louisa tells her parents.

His pleasant mood dissolved (destroyed, and by his daughter!), Jack settles down to getting really drunk, to inveighing against his more abstract scapegoats: the Northern liberal press (*PM*), Mr. Roosevelt and especially Eleanor, the labor unions, Jews.

Caroline and Kenneth both are quiet.

Kate begins to talk as soon as they get up to Louisa's room. They sit across from each other on the ruffled twin beds, removing shoes and clothing. Louisa is aware of a heavy warning in her stomach.

"You know, that John Jeffreys is really amazing," says Kate. "I had no idea—"

"He's cute." This is a word Louisa almost never uses, and it is not at all right for John.

"Oh, well, cute. But he's so intelligent. I mean he has a really original mind."

"Oh, really?" Confused, Louisa realizes that this is not at all what she expected (or wanted) to hear.

"Well, yes. You won't tell anyone? He was saying that he doesn't want to go to college at all; he thinks it would be incredibly silly—a real waste of time, all that fraternity stuff."

At her dressing table Louisa has begun to twist her hair into pin curls that are speared with bobby pins. All the girls at that time go through the ritual every night, and they worry about how it will be when they are married, what with bobby pins and all. "Well?" Louisa asks. She is thinking that so far John doesn't sound exactly brilliant to her.

"You know what he really wants to do? You won't tell anyone?"

"No. What?"

"He wants to join the Navy soon. Or maybe the merchant marine, and go all around the world. Don't you think he looks eighteen?"

"Sure. But suppose we get into the war?"

"John doesn't think we will."

"God, I certainly do." Louisa is rubbing Noxema into her flawless (and unappreciated) skin.

Kate's magic lotion is Calomine, which gives her the look of a clown. "Well, he's really fascinating to talk to," she says.

Having been braced for high romance with glimmerings of sex, Louisa finds this intellectual enthusiasm almost unbearable. God, this is probably the way Kate talks about *her*. Why does she need another friend?

Heedless, Kate goes on: "I don't see why boys can't be friends with girls, do you? I mean without all that silly stuff, sex and all that. John asked me to go for a walk with him tomorrow."

"Oh, really?"

Kate and John Jeffreys walk all through that spring, through warm pine woods where pink or white dogwood suddenly flowered, past the small waterfall that tumbled over dark smooth rocks with anemones in the crevices —down the stream lined with thick caves of blossoming honeysuckle, down to the swollen creek. They walk and they talk about everything that has ever been in either of their minds: books they have read, music (one of the things that John would like to be is a musician in a band), God, their parents, their friends, school, the future, the meaning of life. They are friends, with none of that silly stuff.

And Louisa and Kate remain good friends, too, except that Kate understands that Louisa does not want to hear much about John. They see each other somewhat less, because of the time that John takes up with Kate. Left more to herself, Louisa writes more poetry; she does small intricate drawings of flowers.

Then, one hot night in May, John and Kate, who have never on purpose touched each other, meet in a kiss, and everything changes. They have been to the movies, and they walk home. The night sky is dark blue, and hung with huge dim clouds, and dim white shrubbery blooms beside the highway, smelling thin and sweet. John and Kate loiter, idly talking. Then, in a grove of flowering quince, at the edge of Kate's yard, they stop—stop walking and talking, too—and they look at each other. Simultaneously they move toward each other, and their closed mouths softly meet, and they stay together for incredible moments.

Parting, they are speechless, out of breath. Their blood races.

John says, "I don't want to sound silly or anything, but I like you very much."

"John, I love you!"

"I love you, too."

Another kiss. Kate feels her whole being focused in her mouth—nothing else of her exists, only her mouth that is pressed against John's mouth.

After that they kiss a lot. On their walks they stop in a stand of pines, and kiss. Certain places along their roads become landmarks: here we stopped (and now stop) to kiss. Beside a grapevine swing, near the waterfall—at a blind bend on the road to Morgan's Bend. (Later, when her heart is broken, Kate will go back to those places by herself, making desperate magic wishes.)

"Louisa, I really should tell you something important: John and I are madly in love with each other."

"Oh, really?" But Louisa is interested; she sees mad love as a change for the better.

It is another hot night. The two girls are sitting on the edge of Louisa's pool again, but this time they are wearing their bathing suits (The night they discovered "sex appeal" was the last time they went in without suits—but why?)

"When he kisses me—I just—I don't know!" Kate exclaims, and she laughs a little breathlessly.

"Is that all you do, just kiss?"

"Well, yes. What do you mean?"

"Don't you want to—you know—go all the way?" Lacking words, Louisa made this last ironic, and now they both laugh.

"God, I don't know!" Kate gasps at what is almost a new idea.

Louisa goes away for the summer to a girls' camp in New Hampshire, while Jack and Caroline take a cruise to Mexico.

The two girls write to each other often.

Kate to Louisa: "It's been so hot, hot hot and hotter, and the town is empty and dusty, and I miss you! John is at Myrtle Beach with his parents and I have no one to talk to at all, or walk or anything. Damn!"

Louisa to Kate: "Camp is really boring this year. Everyone seems so young, but sailing is really quite a lot of fun."

Kate: "John is back, thank God! I have been thinking about something you asked me last spring, but you probably don't remember. And Louisa, yesterday some of the girls and I were talking and we decided to start a Sub-Deb Club. You know, have meetings and give parties and we can invite boys. And we want you to be a member. Guess who won't be invited to join, you get one guess. Hint hint—her initials are S. MacD."

Louisa: "Thank God, only two more weeks. Sub-Deb Club? Doesn't that imply later being a deb? But okay, I'll join. We're all so bored here that some of us have put peroxide in our hair. Miss Welch is *furious*."

Kate's parents, Jane and Charles Flickinger, are frantically stylish people, originally from Milwaukee. They both have small incomes from sources that they do not care to mention (a brewery, some cornfields in Iowa). From time to time, Charles works as a designer, and Jane collects and refinishes antiques. Charles designed their remodeled house in Hilton, the old Hemenway house. Where there had been a dank but not very deep cellar, he put in a "game room" that led out to a flagstone terrace. The bar is there, of course, and sometimes Jane and Charles entertain down there, with sophisticated after-dinner drinks made from dark liqueurs.

Kate keeps her record collection in that room, and some of her books. Sometimes on rainy or even unbearably hot afternoons (the game room has kept some of the cellar's cool), Louisa and Kate spend long hours down there, leafing through Jane Flickinger's old *New Yorker*s or *Vogue*s.

In the first days of her friendship with John Jeffreys, sometimes they, too, spend hours in that room, talking and listening to records. And after they kiss and fall in love, Kate imagines that they will spend even more time there, alone, dancing together in the private dark, kissing on the broad soft corduroy-covered sofa.

But after dancing for a while, slowly, pressed together ("Mood Indigo"), John pulls away from her, and he says, "Come on, how about a walk? We could go into Bowman's for Cokes."

"There're Cokes upstairs in the icebox."

"But it's really pretty out. Come on."

Then, on an August night when John and Kate had planned to go to the movies, there comes a crashing thunderstorm. Sheets of water flail against the windows, and Kate's parents call from a party twenty miles away to say that they're staying overnight.

"You'll be all right, ducks?"

"Of course. Have a good time."

John says, "Maybe I'd better go on home, then."

"In this rain? God, are you crazy? Come on, let's go down and put on some records."

"In the Mood."

"Tuxedo Junction."

"Little Brown Jug."

"Flying Home."

John chooses these records; he puts them on, and they dance their own practiced, graceful jitterbug. Back and forth, toward and away from each other, twirling apart and then together again. But not very close together; the music is too fast for that. They clown around, burlesquing the steps and laughing a lot.

Then, "God!" Kate cries out. "I'm exhausted. Can't we have something soothing now?" And she flops onto the broad sofa. She throws off her shoes (brown sandals) and draws up bare smooth brown legs beneath her full red-and-white checked skirt.

"Moonlight Serenade."

John comes and sits beside her.

She lies back on the sofa. When John turns, he sees that her breasts have slipped sideways, so that the hard nipples point out. He leans down to her and they kiss—for the first time horizontal.

The kiss lasts and their bodies press together. Then Kate's frantic whisper in his ear: "John, let's take our clothes off and—do everything."

He pulls back violently, roughly, away from her. "You're crazy, you don't know what you're saying—"

"But I love you!"

"Love—you don't know what you're talking about."

(Of course he is right: how can she know anything about the wild instincts and the stronger repressions in a fifteen-year-old small-town Southern white Protestant boy in 1941? She only knows that his dark brown eyes are beautiful, knows the tender back of his neck as a place to kiss, and her body knows that they want each other.)

Adjusting his clothes, John gets up and goes into the bathroom.

Kate smooths her skirt and sits up. Fortunately she is

better able to say what she feels than would a more repressed and emotionally convoluted girl (Louisa).

"You make me feel awful," she tells John when he comes back. "Like I'd said some terrible thing."

"No." In control of himself now, he is still terribly conflicted. Wars rage in his mind, and in his blood. As an escape, he chooses Southern charm, a thing that all his life he has watched men do. "You Yankee girls are just too much for me," he says.

This is an old joke between them, but it is almost too appropriate for the present occasion, and Kate's smile is a little wan.

Outside the storm has passed, and John soon goes on home.

Fall. First a long Indian summer of warm deep blue days and gently cool nights, succeeded by a brilliant October: the blue air electrified, and the leaves crimson and gold on oaks and maples and grapevines out in the woods, and blue smoke rising straight up from Negro cabins out in the country.

Louisa has come home from camp with a deep New Hampshire tan and a white-blond streak in her hair, which seem to make her hazel eyes lighter, too; they are pale green against her dark skin.

"Louisa's got downright pretty," some of the girls who have known her all her life (Snubby to Betty Sue) now say to each other.

"She has always been very pretty," says loyal Kate.

The boys tease Louisa. "Hey, blondie—hey, dizzy blonde! Hey, Louisa, what's your secret formula?"

Louisa laughs and blushes and feigns annoyance. She is confused and exhilarated by so much attention.

. . .

The Sub-Deb Club meets at Kate's house, in the game room (where she still sometimes comes with John, but not for long, and they don't kiss there). The girls play records and drink Cokes and R.C.'s, and giggle and try to decide what to do with themselves.

At last someone says, "This would be a terrific room for a party," and they all seize on that. It becomes instantly apparent that a party is what they had wanted all along.

After some discussion, rules are established: each girl will invite one and only one boy; therefore there will be no stags and no cutting in. Couples can double-break on each other, if anyone wants to do that. They will all chip in on the punch and cookies.

Louisa stays on after the other girls go; she helps Kate carry bottles and crumby plates upstairs. Often left alone by her servantless and partygoing parents, Kate is very domestic; she made all the brownies for that meeting, and now she cleans up the kitchen until it is shining. ("Kate is going to make some man a marvelous wife," her mother sometimes sighs.)

They go back downstairs, and Kate puts on a record.

"Deep Purple."

"The trouble is," Louisa brings out, "I really don't know who to ask."

Passionately thinking of John, who should have called her last night and did not, Kate still ponders her friend's problem. "How about Richard?"

"Richard Trowbridge? But I've known him all my life. He'd think I'd gone crazy."

"No. I think he likes you."

"But I'd feel so silly. Calling him up."

Kate muses. "Give it a while. It might somehow work

out that you don't have to call. Like sometime at school." She looks out the back windows, past the terrace to a cluster of scarlet maples, young and very straight. "God, what a fall," she says. "A real Thomas Wolfe October. 'The singing and the gold'?"

"Yes." But Louisa is in one of her least poetic moods. "Wait till Snubby hears about the party." And she laughs.

Kate is right. One gaudy afternoon in late October, as Louisa is leaving school, walking down the wide front steps, Richard appears from nowhere at her side. "Hey, blondie, you walking home?"

"Yes—"

"Okay if I join you?"

"Okay—sure."

"I need to stretch my legs before basketball season," he somewhat unconvincingly explains, as though, since he lives in the opposite direction, his walking home with her required an explanation.

In a rather desultory way they talk about school (how boring), the teachers (how stupid), and he tells her that when he is old enough to drive next year his parents are buying him a car, but he isn't quite sure what kind he wants. "I was thinking about a little coupe with, you know, a rumble seat?"

"Oh, they're cute!" Louisa hears this uncharacteristic word (and tone) issue from her own lips, but she doesn't pay much attention.

Arrived at her house, they do not go inside; instead they walk slowly in a direction away from the house. Neither of them mentions the fact that as children they often played together here, and also at Richard's house—children of friends, brought unwillingly together for the convenience of parents.

"Do you ride much?" asks Richard as they pass the stable.

"No, not really."

"Why not? Don't you like to?"

His tone is kindly, and she tells him the truth, but she tells it with art. "The truth is"—and she looks at him (artfully)—"actually I'm afraid of horses."

"Oh? I sort of like that." He chuckles.

"You do?"

"Yes, I think it's sort of nice, in a girl. I'd hate a really *horsy* girl." He laughs.

Arrived at the pool, they sit on the edge. Some yellow oak leaves have drifted down to the water; slowly they sail across the dark surface with no ripples.

Offhandedly (very) Louisa says, "Oh, I don't know if you'd want to come, but some of us have this club—"

A new girl in school. A tiny, mouse-haired girl named Mary Beth Williamson, from South Carolina. She seems shy, she speaks almost inaudibly, in the longest drawl, and her wide gray eyes look scared. She wears flouncy, tight-waisted dresses that have an old-fashioned look.

"God, the poor little thing!" Kate says.

"I don't know—I think she looks dishonest," says Louisa quite unreasonably.

"Louisa, you are crazy."

"There are certain kinds of Southern-girl bitchiness that you still don't understand," says Louisa, in her superior way.

"Well, I think she looks pitiful. I think we ought to ask her to join the club. Think what a blow that would be to Snubby," she cleverly adds.

Kate's kind intentions and reasoning prevail; even Louisa guiltily votes to let Mary Beth in.

"You all are so *nice*!" says Mary Beth when told about the club and the forthcoming party. "But who-all would I *ask*? I don't know any of these here boys." (She drags out "boys" tenderly, adding several vowels.) She says, "Maybe I'll just ask that little old Burton Knowles. He's the one closest to my size." And she giggles softly (and Louisa thinks: Uh-*huh*).

"Burton's very bright," Louisa tells Mary Beth.

"I always did like smart boys."

Mary Beth at the party is something of a surprise. A pink angora sweater, cinched in at the waist with a wide patent belt, and pink lipstick (the other girls don't wear lipstick yet) combine to make her look a great deal less mousy.

Louisa is getting along well with Richard. On the way to the party, in the back seat of his father's Buick, he took her hand and held it. That touch mysteriously stirred her, so that she is still excited, and she laughs a lot.

And how nice it is to have no stags at the dance—no extra boys to smile at, hoping that they'll cut in.

"There's a French song called '*Auprès de ma blonde*,'" Richard tells Louisa. "My mother has it on a record. But I won't tell you the rest of it." He laughs.

"Why not?" She laughs, too, looking up at him, at his blond head near hers.

"Oh, maybe sometime, My blonde. I like that," he says. "The way it sounds."

Of course he isn't stupid!

Louisa watches John and Kate double-break on Burton Knowles and Mary Beth. (Whose idea was that—kindly

Kate's or John's?) She watches as John begins to dance with Mary Beth, spinning her out on the floor. Louisa watches John watching Mary Beth, and she knows when she last saw that look on John's face, that amused curiosity: at last year's dance, John watching Kate.

As the dance ends, John's hands clasp Mary Beth's small waist, easily spanning it, and Louisa hears him say, "Aren't you afraid you'll break off in two pieces?"

(God, and she used to think John was intelligent!)

The wide scared-rabbit eyes. "No, I'm not scared. Not scared of breaking, anyway."

Because Louisa and Kate live so close to each other, Richard walks Louisa home. Exhilarated, in the crisp and vibrant dark, they hurry along, still talking, still animated from the dance.

"That room is really super," Richard says. "I'd like to have a house with a room like that sometime, wouldn't you?"

Is he asking her to marry him? "Oh, yes!"

(And later will he kiss her? Should she let him, or is it too soon? Does it count that she has known him a long time? These are good Sub-Deb questions, for which she has no answers.)

"Who's that new girl?" Richard asks.

Warily: "Her name's Mary Beth Williamson. She's from South Carolina."

"How come she was there?"

"Oh, Kate felt sorry for her, and thought she ought to be invited."

"Kate's nice."

"Oh, yes, she's really nice." (They have both forgotten that last year Richard was madly in pursuit of Kate.)

"But I don't know about that Mary Beth," says

Richard. "Seems like she's—she's some sort of a *type*, you know?" Richard is a snob; by "a type" he means "common," which is the word his mother would have used.

"Oh, yes!" Louisa says. How could she ever have thought him stupid?

Lights flood the huge sprawling Calloway house, but there is no one home.

Louisa and Richard go around to the side of the house, and up the stairs to the porch.

Actually the night is quite cold, but they don't notice that. Stars flicker between the leaves of a giant oak that stands next to the porch.

On the wide cushioned wicker sofa, Louisa and Richard sit several self-conscious inches apart. Still in the spirit of the party (although another mood is now upon them both), Richard laughs and turns to her and says, "You want to make a bet?"

She is curious. "Sure."

"I'll bet I can kiss you without touching you."

Softly, "Oh, really?"

They turn to face each other. Their arms reach and clasp, their mouths meet. For a long time.

"I guess I lost the bet," says Richard, and they both laugh before kissing again.

The following week, in which November begins, there is an unexpected heavy snow.

Fall is over, and almost that easily everything has changed. Waking on Monday to a thick silent world of snow, and waking in love with Richard (since she loves to kiss him, she must be in love with him, mustn't she? Of course she is), Louisa anticipates a beautiful, crystal walk to school through the snow. She telephones Kate, who sounds strange.

"I've got a cold," Kate explains. Then, hesitantly, "You might tell John that he could call during study hall if he wants to. I mean, I'm pretty much by myself."

At school, as though everyone were suddenly ten years younger, the boys lob snowballs at the girls, and the girls squeal and cover their eyes and ears with mittened hands. Louisa watches John throw a couple of snowballs at Mary Beth, whose useless mittens are white Angora (of course), a couple at Snubby, a couple at her—so he distributes his favors. Richard throws snowball after snowball at Louisa. "Hey, blondie, you've got snow all over your hair."

The lazy sound of his voice excites Louisa—she is in love!

During study hall, she covertly starts a poem about Richard, about an autumn night. Stars. A breeze. But popular-song words get in the way. This is the story of a starry night. She crumples the paper and stares out the window at the shining snow, the brilliant icicles.

On the way home that afternoon she stops off at Kate's house. Kate in her dark blue robe, red hair pulled back, red nose. They go downstairs and put on some records.

"Getting Sentimental Over You."

"Body and Soul."

"More Than You Know."

Kate laughs. "God," she says, "no one would guess what's on your mind." But her voice is harsh (her cold?). "Did you get a chance to talk to John?"

"Oh, God, I forgot."

"That's okay. He'll probably call tonight."

"Kate, I'm really sorry."

"It's okay." Kate looks curiously at her friend. "You really had a good time with Richard?"

"Well, yes. A lot better than I thought."

"That's terrific!" Then, instantly, Kate's enthusiasm fades. "But boys are really funny, aren't they?"

Tentatively: "How do you mean?"

"Oh, I don't know."

That night Richard telephones Louisa. Some of the boys have decided to have a sort of sledding party on Friday night, he says. They'll coast all over the golf course which is notorious for its hills. Could she come—with him?

Of course, she'd love to.

A pause, and then his voice, softly, "I wish Friday night was right now, do you?"

"Oh, yes!"

On Wednesday another fall of snow has deepened the roadside banks, and Kate is still not back at school. In the afternoon Louisa stops off at her house. Kate answers the door, and Louisa has a curious sense that she is both cured of her cold and seriously ill (of what?). And Kate says, "I'm okay, I just didn't feel like going to school." Then her eyes fill with tears and she says, "Come on, let's go downstairs."

But when they sit down to talk, Kate's tears are gone, and angrily she says, "Well, I really made an ass of myself that time. I called John and said I wanted to see him; would he come over? Was that such a terrible thing to do? Well, I guess it was."

John, with the furtive look of a man accused by a woman, came to see her. Yesterday afternoon. At first he said he didn't know what she was talking about. Nothing had changed. He had been busy. The snow. Basketball practice. But then he reversed himself and made a speech that sounded long-prepared. They had been getting too serious about each other, for people their age, he said. Of course he still liked her, she was a terrific girl, but shouldn't they both see other people—sometimes?

"God," Kate says to Louisa. "I couldn't believe it was *John*, saying all that dumb stuff. John is so in*tell*igent. He sounded like something out of some dumb advice column. Like a Sub-Deb column." She laughs harshly.

Kate's anger makes it harder for Louisa to respond; in her own heightened emotional state she could more readily answer sorrow—she was prepared to weep with Kate. Weakly she says, "That's too bad."

Of course it doesn't really matter what Louisa says or does not say.

Kate goes on. "I had this terrible feeling that I was too much for him, you know? And now he's made me feel all heavy and serious, when we had so much *fun*."

"God, I'm really sorry."

"Obviously what he means is that he wants to see that drippy little Mary Beth. You were so right about her."

"I guess." But Louisa is becoming impatient; she wants to be alone, and to savor her own love affair.

"I really feel lousy," Kate says. "Honestly, maybe you'd better go. My cold must be coming back or something."

By Friday, even more snow has fallen on the town (miraculously, for so early in November)—on the golf course, everywhere. And Louisa is well embarked on what is to be a lifetime occupation, or preoccupation: the enshrouding of any man at all in veils and layers of her own complexity, so that the love object himself is nearly lost. Who is Richard? By the time he comes to her door, blond and smiling and happy to see her, he is also innumerable other people, with whom she has imaginatively acted out a hundred passionate episodes.

(It is the following spring, and a new girl has come to school, a more voluptuous Mary Beth, and Richard suddenly abandons Louisa, just as John has left Kate. It is five years later and she and Richard get married. This country gets into the war and Richard is killed. It is many years later, at a party in New York: Louisa is a famous poet-painter-actress and Richard comes up to her at a party and asks if she remembers him. It is any time at all and she and Richard make love in some warm and dark and very private place.)

Since the country club and golf course border Jack Calloway's land, Louisa and Richard walk along the narrow shoveled path, between high banks of snow, in the starry crystal dark. As soon as they are out of sight of her parents' house, he takes her hand and they walk silently, until Richard says, "You know, something funny came up. John told me he's bringing along that Mary Beth tonight."

Louisa's heart sickens and shrinks, but loyalty prompts her to make as little of this as possible. "Well, Kate's still home with her cold," she tells him.

"She is? Well, that's different. I guess."

Thus, from the beginning, her knowledge of Kate's pain adds a melancholy depth to Louisa's love affair, or perhaps Kate's suffering touches an important chord already present in Louisa. A few minutes later, when Richard stops at a bend in the path and they kiss, some part of Louisa feels a thrill of pain, and she thinks of Kate and John, who also kissed, perhaps at that very bend, before the snow.

"God," Richard says. "You're fun to kiss."

She dimly feels that this is not quite what he should have said, but at that moment his presence is stronger, more powerful, than the dark workings of her own mind.

In the distance, then, they see the pillared, well-lit

country club, and the white smooth undulations of the golf course, the bluish snow. Their friends are there with sleds, all gathered near the club's front steps. Mary Beth with John, Snubby with someone tall but indistinguishable. Other couples.

Tightening his grip on her hand, Richard says, "God, this should really be fun."

"Oh, yes!" Louisa says.

Two / 1945

Now Louisa's father is in Virginia; he is in a sanatorium, being treated with electric shock for a depression. She is not; she is in Cambridge with Norm Goldman, on a corduroy sofa. They have just fallen in love. She has been crying because she is upset about her father's shock treatment, which her mother has just written a long letter to tell her about. So far (she and Norm do not know each other very well), he finds her tears both touching and attractive. "It really upsets you, doesn't it," he says, and he strokes her long just-curled brown hair.

Norm is the first of a series of those very intelligent, affectionate, and mildly but interestingly evasive Jewish boys who imagine that being gentile makes Louisa stronger than their mothers (she eventually marries Michael, to whom Norman introduces her—Michael with the worst of all possible mothers); they imagine that she will protect them with her Episcopal magic.

They are in Cambridge; it is April, 1945. Norm's room in Lowell House, at Harvard. A soft April by the

Charles heightened by tremors from the war. Norm's touch is soft. He is a thin, dark boy, in khaki pants and a crisp seersucker coat. He is 4-F because of a bad ear. He has taken off his tie, and some thin black hair shows at his neck. He wears horn-rimmed glasses. The curtains on his window are in five shades of gray, light to dark, and there are reproductions of Cézanne, Dufy, and Klee on his walls. He is studying architecture at the School of Design. He is right; the idea of her father having shock treatment upsets Louisa very much, although she is not sure what electric shock is.

And she is not sure why she is so upset; she would have said that she did not like her father, Jack, who owns vast acres of tobacco fields, who drinks too much and makes loud awful jokes about Jews and Negroes and Yankees. She does not remember liking him at all since she was very young and he taught her to swim, one summer at Virginia Beach, before they built the pool at home. She wonders if it is an idea, the idea called Father, that moves her to tears. (She does not like her mother much, either, not yet—poor languid Caroline.)

She has stopped crying and she and Norm begin to kiss. His mouth tastes of tobacco.

Norm believes that Louisa is what she presents herself as: a pretty, tall girl, walking across the Yard in loafers and white athletic socks, a pleated gray flannel skirt and a large pink sweater, pearls—a girl who laughs a lot, who knows a lot of people and says "Hi" as she walks from Widener to Emerson Hall, where he is waiting before the class on the English lyric, 4-B. He does not know that she is really in love with the professor, himself a poet, a tall blond man in very English clothes, an English voice. The professor reminds Louisa a great deal of her father's psychiatrist, Kenneth Mills, a great family friend.

One night (also at Virginia Beach) Louisa went swimming alone with the psychiatrist. (Who on earth allowed that? A nubile eighteen-year-old girl and a forty-one-year-old thickening man.) And in the hot black night, on the hard sand, she revealed to him (since he was a psychiatrist) what was ruining her with guilt and confusion: she had been making love (is that the word she used?—no matter) with a young doctor in Boston, an intern at Mass. General, whom she thinks does not really like her very much, certainly is not in love with her. With that confession she and the doctor fell upon each other wildly. Their passion was not consummated, so to speak, that night—in fact, not until much later (during, in fact, her love affair with Norm Goldman), when he (the psychiatrist) came to Boston and in his room at the Ritz there was a violent hurried collision of their flesh, if anyone calls that a consummation—hurried because he expected his wife back from shopping, and she did come back, just after his zipping up and Louisa's smoothing down of clothes. The wife and Louisa never liked each other, but they were strongly linked as enemies. "Hey, there, Louisa, you're looking mighty pretty. You young girls are so cute without any lipstick. I could never get away with it—not that I'd want to try."

Norm knows none of this, not about the intern and certainly not about her father's psychiatrist. In fact, he thinks she is a virgin, and all spring they go on necking on his sofa, squirming against each other. Once, during a Fête Charrette for architectural students at which they got drunk, they necked for a long time on the back steps of the Fogg Museum. Now near the steps of Emerson they hold hands, in the April sun, in front of everyone. Norm says, "How about tonight? Want to catch a flick?"

"I'm really sorry. I promised to have dinner with some people from home. My father's doctor, in fact."

"Oh." He wonders: is she not asking him along because he is Jewish?

"At least I'll find out how he is—my father," she says, meaning that it is to be a private conversation. "His wife is awful. A real Southern bitch."

Louisa has reason to believe that her father is having an affair (unconsummated?) with the wife. She wonders: Is she upset about his shock treatments?

At dinner, in the big white Ritz dining room, they do not talk much about Louisa's father. In those elegant surroundings the subject suddenly seems tasteless. Also (and with good reason) they are all too nervous with each other for intimate conversation. Once the wife says, "I do think your daddy's getting a whole lot better." The doctor murmurs but does not comment; after all, he is the one who has sent Jack to the sanatorium for shock. They ask Louisa how she likes school, and how she likes living up here among all these Yankees. She answers, more or less, but by now she is thinking about Norm.

(Much later, in San Francisco, she tries to tell her own doctor about all this, but it becomes literary. "It's all so Southern, right out of Faulkner, all this incest stuff. Screwing my father's psychiatrist instead of him. Jews instead of Negroes, do you suppose?" By then Louisa is having an affair with a white Southern bigot, betraying her husband, good Michael, and her daughter Maude for a man whom in most ways she loathes. She does not tell her doctor about that man. The doctor is a liberal.)

Louisa's mother is an intellectual, of sorts. Caroline. She explains in her long typed letters that shock treatment is a great help to her father, that he even asks for it. "It alleviates some of that awful Presbyterian guilt," she tells

Louisa. (She is an Episcopalian who secretly believes that she has married beneath her.) She is usually quite depressed herself, is Caroline, what with one thing and another. Louisa has reason to believe that her mother has a sort of crush on the psychiatrist. But Louisa's father is the one who is getting the shocks. After he has been in Boston, Louisa telephones the doctor, weeping with despair and what she calls love, across all those miles, and he tries to explain to her what electric shock is. Electrodes are placed. Convulsions. Her father asks for this? Jack?

One afternoon in Cambridge some old friends come to see Norm: Michael Wasserman and his girl. Michael is blond, with a broad Slavic face and a wide loose mouth. The girl is small and dark, voluptuous, assured. It is clear that they are sleeping together—they are having an affair; this fact, and their contrasting looks, makes them strongly attractive to Louisa. Michael says "fuck" a lot (as though he were very sexy) and this, too, seems exotic; it is not a word that Norm would use, and God knows not any of the nice Southern boys at home.

Michael talks a great deal about his parents. (Such a bad sign! Later Louisa recognizes how much was contained in that first meeting.)

"My mother went up to the attic where I was supposedly sleeping," Michael says. "With blankets or some goddam thing. Actually she's very prurient. And guess what? I'm not there. Her logical conclusion was that I was in my own room, where my house guest was supposedly sleeping." He laughs, and the girl smiles self-consciously: she is not quite assured enough for this intimate exposure.

"I guess I'm not supposed to get laid at home," says Michael, with satisfaction (smiling his false-sexy smile).

"Get laid" is another new phrase.

Louisa thinks he is interesting.

Michael likes her, too. "Did anyone ever tell you that you've got terrifically sexy legs?" he asks.

As a matter of fact, no one has.

(In San Francisco, later, she and her own psychiatrist also wonder if she would have been "happier" if she had married Norm Goldman. But she at least knows that she is too crazy to be married to anyone, except of course to her analyst. If he loved her, all her problems would be solved; that would prove that she is not crazy. As it is, she amuses him with the Yiddish words that she has learned over the years—why is it always so funny for non-Jews to speak Yiddish?—and with what he takes to be jokes. When he asked why she thought she needed analysis, she said because she hated her father and she thought about hating him all the time. He asked why, and she said she supposed because she was in love with him. He laughed, reassuring them both that Louisa is not insane, making them both think the doctor can help her. If he knew how really crazy she is, he would not like her at all.)

"Michael liked you a lot," Norman tells her.

"Oh, really?" Cool Louisa.

"Yes, I could tell. I'll bet he calls you."

(Why should she be upset about her father being shocked? Why again and again? He is a manic-depressive; her mother has explained that it is cyclic.)

Three / 1947

"Jews are not welcome there," says Mrs. Wasserman, Michael's mother and Louisa's mother-in-law to be, with one of her massively self-pitying sighs. She is speaking of a resort in New Hampshire which one of her two non-Jewish guests has just mentioned—guests, actually, of her two sons. Since this is in the mid-forties, her sentence has nightmare echoes of Hitler and Nazi camps, as she has intended that it should. Also, everyone is embarrassed.

And her remark has other, unintended results. Barbara Spaulding, the guest of Mrs. Wasserman's thin, elegant, and homosexual son Martin, is confirmed in the prevailing, if fairly gentle, distaste for Jews of her social class, which is fringe-upper. Barbara is blond and stylish. "Wasserman," such an ugly name with its suggestion of urine specimens, and Mrs. Wasserman's considerable ugliness, and the bad dinner which Barbara is being served (a dinner lavishly praised by the family) all combine with that embarrassing remark to make her acutely uncomfortable. Much later in life, when her style has rather hardened, Barbara will be known to say, "Unfortunately the first Jews I ever met were horrible. Absolutely revolting people, gross, except for Martin. I certainly can't blame him for changing that name, poor thing."

Chewing at her overdone roast beef, Barbara tries not to look accusingly at Martin. She is married; her husband, Eliot, is overseas in the Navy. She has some money and a small apartment on the wrong side of Beacon Hill, and not much to do. Idle and lonely, she has chosen to take some courses at the Fogg Museum, at Harvard, where Martin is working. Martin—aesthetic, and safe—is a satisfactory friend, as she is for him. They share a taste for Henry James over innumerable cups of coffee at St. Clair's, and in nice weather they bicycle around Cambridge. In speaking of his family Martin has emphasized their Russian rather than their Jewish character; Barbara has imagined a rather gentle, Turgenev atmosphere, with backgrounds of pleasant music, and a pervasive tone of warmth and generosity, and perhaps an interestingly exotic taste as to décor. And of course exceptional food. At that instant in her life Barbara welcomes novelty; she is to become more rigid in her tastes.

The other guest is pale dark Louisa Calloway, who has mentioned the resort and who now blushes terribly and decides that somehow she must become Jewish; she must marry Michael, the fat asthmatic son with whom she has been quarreling all afternoon. She wants to bear that name. Also, in her confusion, she thinks that if Michael would love her enough to marry her, he would be less critical of her, and that his acceptance will somehow erase those defects he perpetually criticizes: her tastes in books and music and movies, her clothes, her small breasts.

"My wife has always been an exceptional cook," says Mr. Wasserman in his courtly way to Barbara, whose perfectly stitched shoes and trim ankles he appreciates.

"Well, anyway, it's not at all nice there," babbles Louisa, of the New Hampshire resort. "The lake is shallow and icky on the bottom. We had an awful time there. I wouldn't *want* to go back."

"Michael, do me a favor—have some more peas," says Michael's mother. She is informed by her instincts that Louisa is dangerous but that if sufficiently ignored she will dissolve, which in time turns out to be quite true: Louisa dissolves into colitis. Mrs. Wasserman is a stupid, childish, completely selfish, and very powerful woman. Her ugliness accuses everyone: her big bulbous nose and small stingy mouth, her pigeon-fat body, her impossible thinning gray hair. She even has a wandering left eye, inherited by her elder son, by Martin, who otherwise ironically resembles his masculine father.

But Michael has turned on Louisa. "Then why were you just saying you wanted to go there?" he asks. He is at M.I.T., studying psychology. He has an excellent, if somewhat laborious, intelligence. He is extremely ambivalent about Louisa, almost as ambivalent as she is about herself.

"I just said the name—it just came to me." She defends herself in her smallest voice. Her instincts impossibly war; she wants to hit Michael in the face, to run away by herself and cry; she wants to be loved by and married to Michael, and accepted as a Jew by all Jews.

In contrast to Barbara, Louisa at this period dresses badly. To conceal, she hopes, inadequate breasts, she buys too large clothes. Tonight she wears a shapeless blue wool that is particularly bad in that pale blue dining room.

Another family myth, along with that of the great cooking, is the myth of Mrs. Wasserman's marvelous "taste." Martin has sustained her in this, as in most things, with an effort far more than he can afford. "She used to do some really nice little watercolors," he has told Barbara, who now looks rather snobbishly around that dreary room. A kinder judgment than hers would have described it as understated. All the furniture is good but none of it superior —those cautious English reproduction antiques—and Barbara has grown up in a family collection of real American antiques. Carefully framed Piranesi prints ornament the walls. On the sideboard are two large silver (reproduction) Paul Revere bowls and a cut-glass decanter that is never used. (Barbara's grandmother has an original Revere pewter bowl, which Barbara is to inherit.) "Handsome" is the favorite family word for describing approved objects. Martin and his mother shop together. "Mm, they're handsome," they murmur of the Federal sconces in an antique-store window.

Michael's version of his mother is that she is "earthy." "It's her saving grace," he has told Louisa, who knows that she herself is not earthy. "She really likes a good dirty joke, you know? She really *gets* it." Michael underlines words in order to take possession of them, to insure that they take on his and only his sense of them. Thus his mother's "getting" dirty jokes becomes a unique act.

Now Mrs. Wasserman gives what Louisa supposes to be her earthy laugh. "Martin had a good time one summer at a camp in New Hampshire, didn't you, Marty?"

Both sons laugh, Martin nervously, with a sort of giggle, and Michael with his usual high wheezing cackle.

"Sarah!" says Mr. Wasserman.

Laughter subsides slowly, Mrs. Wasserman's last. She wipes a tear of laughter from one fat cheek, and sighs again.

Louisa has been told in some detail about the summer when Martin was seduced by a counselor at a camp in New Hampshire; Michael finds his brother's homosexuality an absorbing topic. But Louisa has not been told that it is a family joke, and she is not quite sure how to react. She smiles weakly and earns a look of violent reproof from Mr. Wasserman, who turns again to Barbara.

"It must be hard for you, Mrs. Spaulding," he says in his mellifluous Edwardian voice that almost disguises his innate authoritarianism, as well as his furtive lusts. "Living all alone, with your husband overseas."

Confronted with Martin's homosexuality (Martin, in a fit of exhibitionistic despair, had once brought a sailor home to bed), Mr. Wasserman had said, "I understand from your mother that you are homosexual. In that case I expect you to be continent." Thus he Edwardianly removed himself from the situation—his wife, not he, had made the discovery—and from his son. He likes to read lurid detective magazines but he always tears the covers off.

Coldly Barbara says what they all know, that she is studying at the Fogg, and everyone, including Mr. Wasserman, respects her the more for her hauteur.

"I'm writing my thesis on T. S. Eliot," Louisa —unasked—announces. "It's really exciting. I'm almost done."

"T. S. Eliot is an anti-Semite," says Mrs. Wasserman, who passes as an intellectual among her friends, as well as in her family.

"Well, yes, but not in all the poems, and he is sort of a great poet anyway, sort of," says Louisa. "Actually I wanted to write about Karl Shapiro but they wouldn't let me."

"An anti-Semite and a great poet is a contradiction in terms," states Mr. Wasserman.

"Now, Daddy," wheezes Michael. "Most people think that Pound is, and Cummings and Yeats. Don't you have to make a dichotomy—or, rather, an *aff*ective—not *eff*ective, *aff*ective—distinction between—"

"No," says his father.

The Irish maid comes in to clear and to bring the

dessert. Traditionally the family does not talk when she is in the room, partly because anti-Catholicism is a staple of conversation: to be anti-Catholic is to be "liberal" and intellectual. And also they regard her as a somewhat retarded child; they speak to her as one would to a child. "Now, Nellie, you help yourself to some of that roast beef—take all you want!" proffers Nellie's mistress.

"No, mum, I'm not hungry," sniffs Nellie, who hates the food served in this house.

Martin's acute sensibilities exaggerate everything, rather like those of Henry James. Now he imagines that Barbara is having a worse time and reacting much more negatively than she actually is, and for this he is furious at her: how dare she judge his mother? What did she expect, the Princess Casamassima? And, if it came to that, she isn't always so perfectly elegant herself, Mrs. Spaulding from the wrong side of Beacon Hill. He gives her furious looks, his wild eye wandering like his mother's.

Michael has been enormously interested in his own reactions to Louisa's argument with his parents over Mr. Eliot. He is always very interested in how he feels about things; for this he is studying psychology. He masturbates a great deal. He now finds himself very much wanting Louisa to defy them further, and to win. He considers this, running it back and forth, wondering what to make of it. In any case he recognizes that he is very pleased with Louisa. He reaches beneath the table for her leg, so that she jumps and flushes.

Mrs. Wasserman sees everything. "Michael, you're hurting Louisa's leg." It has never once in her life occurred to her not to say what comes into her mind.

Louisa in a tiny voice says, "No, he's not."

"Well, if you like it, do it somewhere else," triumphantly brings out Mrs. Wasserman, with her earthy "saving" laugh.

Dessert, at least, is extremely good. Pale crisp delicately fashioned blintzes with sour cream and strawberry jam. This time everyone is enthusiastic but Mrs. Wasserman, who takes tiny critical bites from her fork. "They're just not right," she sighs.

"Now, Sarah," says her husband.

Barbara looks with considerable sympathy at Louisa—not, one hopes, because Louisa is the only other gentile in the room, Nellie having disappeared. Louisa could have been beautiful if she had only known who she was, and it is at this shadow of beauty that Barbara looks. She imagines Louisa with shorter hair, a little dark pencil on her eyelids, a pale green silk dress.

Mr. Wasserman clears his throat in a jovial way; he is about to announce an amusing occurrence. "Well," he says, "Abrams's wife called in to say that he's having a nervous collapse." He laughs. "One more."

Both guests look puzzled and smile faintly at each other as the family joins his laughter; was this funny?

Laughing richly, Mrs. Wasserman explains. Her husband is head of a large electrical contracting firm. They hire bright young men fresh out of M.I.T., many of whom have nervous breakdowns or lapse into alcoholism. This seems, to the family, a judgment on M.I.T. It is an ancient family joke, unquestionably funny.

"Anyway," concludes Mrs. Wasserman, "I always did think Max Abrams was sort of kikey."

That word sends a literal and violent shock down all Louisa's nerves, so that she cries out, "Don't!"

Everyone looks at her.

"How can you use that word?" she blazes out.

Mrs. Wasserman sniffs. "It's a perfectly good word to describe a certain kind of person," she says, and she repeats the word.

"I can't bear that word!" Louisa gasps out. "How can you? When the most horrible people—when Hitler—"

Michael is thrilled. Mistaking Louisa's hysteria for strength, he imagines that she will ultimately protect him from his mother.

And indeed Mrs. Wasserman is for the moment reduced to a mutter. "I know just as much about Hitler as certain people in this room."

Louisa subsides almost as quickly as she has flared. She sits silently, in panic, having glimpsed herself so out of control, having forgotten the cause. Her stomach clenches and her hands shake. She and Mrs. Wasserman avoid looking at each other for the rest of the meal.

"These pancakes are absolutely divine," says Barbara.

"We call them blintzes," sighs her hostess.

That night, in Louisa's furnished room, she and Michael rather breathlessly decide to get married, and immediately fall to discussing parental reactions.

"God, mother will die!" gasps Michael.

"And mine!"

Also, that night, on Louisa's lumpy brown couch, Michael fails utterly in the act of love.

Enthusiastically she massages his flaccid member. To no avail.

With truly maternal solicitude, he asks, "Do you feel very sexy?"

Once more accused, Louisa bursts into tears.

A few weeks later, over coffee at St. Clair's, Martin tells Barbara that Michael and Louisa are married.

"They simply did it," he says. "We were presented with a *fait accompli*. I must say that Daddy behaved very handsomely. Took everyone out to Locke-Ober's for dinner. Not that it was much fun. Naturally Louisa drank too much and got sick." He makes a vivid sound of disgust.

Barbara has reacted in a variety of ways to the story. Sketchy as it is, his description has forced her presence at a scene that she finds very unattractive. Distaste makes her withdraw from Martin; she looks hopefully about the restaurant. There might always be someone she knows. Her eyes search among the pretty girls, the good-looking officers who are not Eliot.

Martin's wild need for affection and approval has produced in him a sort of talent; he is not only acutely sensitive to others' reactions, but he is also able to beautifully recreate people for themselves; he gives them his version of their persons as presents. Now, sensing Barbara's distaste, he has the sensitivity not to pursue her. He also senses what she herself is not quite aware of: that she misses Eliot too much to be able to hear of any other love affair or marriage, even a sordid one like Michael's and Louisa's. The very gaudiness of postwar Cambridge is making her lonely.

So, after a little interval of quiet, he says, "You know, you really ought to have some pictures made to send to Eliot. That suit is really smashing on you. Why don't you call John Brook?"

He does not normally resort to such obvious ruses, but along with his parents he has been very upset about Michael and Louisa. Evenings at home are passed in heavy gloom, among ponderous sighs and dark predictions.

Also, Martin is being blackmailed by a cabdriver whom he has tried to make on the way home from a movie. Martin hates fags; he likes big brutal men—bullies (reminiscent of his father, he later understands). Blackmail is something he has always expected; it is in the cards. But now he does not know what to do about these threats, in very clear and ugly scrawls. Threats to tell the Boston cops, who do not like Jews, or homosexuals.

Returned to him, Barbara smiles, narrowing hazel eyes, showing perfect, if rather large, teeth.

And that for the moment is all she hears about the marriage.

"You know what would be fun?" says Martin. "Let's bike out to Mt. Auburn Cemetery and find Henry James's tomb. He is there, isn't he?"

Then, a few weeks later, quite by accident and God knows unwelcomely, Barbara overhears a conversation—or, rather, a confrontation—between Michael Wasserman and his mother. Barbara is in the poetry corner of the Harvard Co-op; they are behind her, looking at fiction.

"With no rubbers!" says Mrs. Wasserman, evidently by way of greeting to her son.

"It wasn't raining when I went out this morning." But Michael coughs, as though to agree that she was right, after all; he did need rubbers.

"Michael, I'm telling you, from now on if you don't take care of yourself no one else will."

This heavy innuendo could be a description of Louisa; the "no one," at least for Barbara, conjures up that sad pale presence. Unwilling to hear more of what seems to her extremely low comedy, she turns around.

She is recognized with enthusiasm, perhaps relief, by Michael—with reluctance by his mother.

"You look terrific!" Michael enthuses.

"It's nice to see you again," sniffs Mrs. Wasserman,

and then, to her son, "Don't you think this new edition of James Henry stories would be a handsome gift for Martin's birthday?"

"Mother, it's Henry James."

"James Henry, Henry James—" She makes it clear that she prefers the former combination. Then, "Handsome," she repeats, fingering the leather binding.

She is wearing a black seal coat that Barbara recognizes as being very expensive. But her hair is barely pulled together with big ugly gray pins, her fingernails are dirty and cracked, and there is no powder on her nose. Her unmitigated ugliness is felt as a hostile assault (by Barbara). If she had made the slightest effort—combed her hair, for example—her terrible face might have elicited some compassion.

Boldly Barbara congratulates Michael on his marriage.

"Thanks!" he says vehemently. "And we have a great new apartment. You've got to come up and see it. Say, how about now? Some coffee?"

He is urgent, and uncharacteristically Barbara is carried along, perhaps partly out of a feeling that she is needed as a buffer.

Mrs. Wasserman refuses to come. "No, I have to be getting on home. Nellie needs me," she says, achieving another loaded innuendo: Nellie needs her even if no one else does.

"Oh, Mother, come on. You haven't been up since Louisa put up the curtains."

"I'll come another time. Maybe when Louisa invites me." She laughs with no humor whatsoever.

"Oh, Mother."

"Sunday dinner. You'll remember to come?"

And she is gone, leaving most of the weight of her presence behind her, leaving Barbara and Michael to plod along gray crowded rainy Brattle Street together.

Separated from his mother, Michael can be quite articulate about her deficiencies of character. "She's really been appalling about Louisa," he confides. "Do you know what she said? She said to Louisa, 'We've tried to love you,'" and he perfectly imitates his mother's self-pitying tone, her massive ensuing sigh. "*Tried* to love her," he repeats. "Can you imagine anything worse? To try to love?"

Barbara senses that he is talking to himself, which is an impression that Michael often gives, but she agrees with him anyway. After all, he is right.

"This way," Michael says.

He leads her to the rear of a large white picket-fenced house, and up a double flight of outside stairs. He opens a door, to the dirtiest, messiest room that Barbara has ever seen. The windows cut into the slanted ceiling are small, and on that rainy day the light is dim, but as Barbara gets used to the dimness, the mess looks worse. Books and papers are loosely piled in small stacks, like the droppings of an animal. Against one wall is a tangle of sheets, presumably a bed. In another corner a sink and stove and a small table are piled with dirty pots and dishes. Dead center in the room is a small pair of crystal candlesticks, evidently just unpacked—paper and excelsior are scattered about the dark stained carpet. Distaste chills Barbara; it looks like a room whose inhabitants are mad.

"Louisa must be in the bathroom," Michael tells her; quite unnecessarily he adds, "I guess she didn't feel like cleaning up today."

Sounds of water flushing from an adjoining room confirm his supposition. Then Louisa emerges.

"Honey, we've been wanting to see Barbara again, and here she is!" Michael goes over to nuzzle and then kiss his wife's thin neck; Barbara looks away.

Surprisingly, Louisa is enthusiastic about Barbara's visit. "Oh, *yes*, we haven't seen you since that ghastly dinner, when she said all those awful things. God, wasn't it terrible?" And before Barbara can answer she has turned back to her husband. "Did you see these horrible little candlesticks? God, I couldn't believe them. Our wedding present from your parents." But she sounds more triumphant than outraged.

Michael picks up a candlestick and begins a speech. "You don't understand," he tells Louisa and Barbara. "The gift is determined by the economic status of the recipient. I can just hear my mother, 'A silver service would look out of place in their home.' She buys *dreck* in Filene's basement—she's got trunks full—and every time she says it will make a lovely gift, she means it could have no other possible use. But you should have seen the actual silver service they sent to Cousin Albert when he married a New York Strauss. From Tiffany's, yet."

Unmoved by the astuteness of her husband's analysis, which she has heard before, Louisa continues to hold and regard the other candlestick. "Pure *dreck*," she repeats, with her odd mixture of triumph and wonder and despair.

Barbara does not know that word, but she understands that Louisa is trying to sound Jewish, and she wonders why.

Michael offers to make coffee, which Barbara declines. She would not have dared eat or drink anything that was served in that room.

"My parents have been worse than you could believe," Louisa tells Barbara. "My father. He's been writing horrible letters about never wanting to see Jewish grandchildren, and couldn't I make Michael change his name."

Michael laughs. "Like Martin wants to, and maybe they'd rather I was screwing cabdrivers instead of you."

To this laboriously unfunny remark Barbara reacts directly; at that moment she loves her friend Martin and she loathes his brother. She is not sufficiently sensitive (or kindly) to sense the panic behind Michael's laboriousness, his doomed eagerness to please. (And neither is Louisa.)

Barbara gets up. "I have to go."

"I hope I didn't shock you," says Michael, convincing Barbara that he hoped the contrary.

"I just remembered an appointment," Barbara says, seizing on the most transparent in her repertoire of social untruths.

Louisa grimaces and hurries toward the bathroom.

Partly because she regards it as a gentile holiday, Mrs. Wasserman does not dress for Sunday dinner. She wears a housedress, one of her collection of drab shapeless cotton shifts from what she calls The Basement—Filene's. Sighing, she serves the dry roast chicken.

Louisa cannot eat. Her illness has made her despise all food; she would have chosen to get rid of, rather than to nourish, her body.

"Louisa, you're not eating," says Mrs. Wasserman.

"I'm sorry, I'm not very hungry."

"I suppose you're used to a different kind of food," insinuates her hostess, who correctly regards rejection of her food as a rejection of herself, but who has further (incorrectly) concluded that Louisa is pregnant.

Louisa blushes and excuses herself to go to the bathroom. By this time there is no ambivalence; she is disgusting, she loathes herself.

On Louisa's return, Mrs. Wasserman remarks, in her "earthy" manner, "I should have known there was only one reason for hasty weddings."

Puzzled, almost stupefied, Louisa stares at her, then says, "I think I have colitis."

That changes everything. Mrs. Wasserman is consumingly fond of diseases. Enthusiastically she cries out, "But you poor thing, why didn't you tell me? You must be miserable. You know," she goes on, addressing her whole family, in which Louisa is now for the first time included, "that's interesting. I was just reading about some experiments on colitis patients with ACTH. Cortizone." She turns to Louisa. "How many times a day do you have to go?"

The following spring, after having served in the occupation army, Eliot Spaulding comes home to Boston. To Barbara. And eventually to his father's law firm. Barbara and Eliot are very happy together. For the next few years or so there are a lot of parties, reunions, and weddings all over Boston and up on the North Shore, down in New Haven and New York. They are not as splendid as the parties that now are referred to as "prewar," but they are fun. Barbara and Eliot are very much caught up in all that postwar fun. Busy and quite content, Barbara has no further need or even time for Martin, who would not have fitted in. Although almost.

But she is, or has been, very fond of Martin, and one day on a nostalgic impulse she calls and asks him over for lunch. He accepts eagerly, and arrives with a small bunch of spring flowers. But he looks so badly that Barbara is almost sorry she called him. His face is terribly dark and sallow and drawn, and there are what look like bruises on his neck.

Uneasily they settle with sherry in Barbara's pretty living room, simultaneously aware that neither of them has personal news that can be presented to the other as conversation.

As always, Martin tries very hard. He compliments her on the room, in the new Chestnut Street apartment, skillfully selecting touches which are surely hers: the small Victorian chair in toile, the good framed Klee that he remembers from her old apartment. "It's wonderful to be in a place where there are *no* Lautrec posters," he tells her, laughing as though they were still close friends.

"There do seem to be a lot around," she agrees.

"Droves. As bad as last year's 'Sunflowers' or that Picasso mother."

Finding no other response, or available topic, Barbara asks, "How is your mother?"

"Oh, fine. She's eternal," Martin has forgotten for the moment that Barbara has met his mother, as well as Michael and Louisa. "A rather upsetting thing has happened with my brother, though," he says. "His wife has some awful disease and they tried to treat it with cortisone and the drug made her go crazy. They called it a toxic psychosis. We all think Michael should do something about a divorce."

Actually only Martin thinks Michael should do something about a divorce. Mr. Wasserman is against all divorce; he finds the idea terrifying. What would he do if *he* were free? And Mrs. Wasserman argues that it would be unfair to poor sick Louisa, thus insuring herself against more daughters-in-law.

Barbara notices now that she is feeling worse and worse—both more impatient and more paralyzed, and she has no idea why. The truth is that Martin's depression and his anxiety—he is at the far limits of both—are affecting her, as cold germs or even a bout of yawning might have done.

Sensitive Martin understands what he is doing to her. He is sorry he has come, and he thinks of leaving suddenly, on any pretext at all. He doesn't know what to do, and so he does the worst thing he could have done. He says, "Dear old Barbara, I'm sorry to have come to you in such bad shape. The truth is that I'm in the middle of an absolutely disastrous love affair. Last night he tried to strangle me." Martin smiles and fingers his neck as his large dark eyes fill with tears.

Barbara is horrified. She has of course known that Martin is "queer," but she has not extended this knowledge to include his having love affairs with men, and certainly not men who would try to strangle him. Rather stiffly she says, "I'm terribly sorry, Martin." And then, "Excuse me, I have to see about lunch."

By the time she comes back to say that lunch is ready, Martin has pulled himself together, and though it takes all of his exhausted strength, he talks with most of his old animation, his desperate charm, all during lunch. He has read or somehow heard about various phases of Barbara's new life, a life that is fully as attractive to him as his is repellent to her. He amuses her with gossip, managing to make it "Jamesian" in its subtlety and its discretion, and managing at the same time to suggest that they both know that she is superior to the apparent frivolity of her life. Thus he quiets various doubts that sometimes, if weakly, nag at Barbara's generally cheerful mind. He almost succeeds in making her forget what he earlier said.

But that unfortunate day is, for the moment, the end of their friendship, Barbara's and Martin's. He wisely does not call her to thank her for lunch. And soon afterward he reads that Mr. and Mrs. Eliot Spaulding have moved to San Francisco. (Like many Navy men, Eliot fell in love with that city, and had dreamed of living there.)

And soon after that Martin recovers from his love affair.

Barbara and her husband flourish in San Francisco. In common with most of their class, they survive and pass as very nice people, partly by blocking out or not seeing what is unpleasant: burned Asians, the American poor. Even the mildly "intellectual" phase of Barbara's life has come to an end; she finds that she has less and less time to read. Besides, no one is reading Henry James any more.

And occasionally, when Barbara grows older and makes her remark to the effect that the first Jews she ever met were horrible ("unfortunately"), it is pointed out to her by more thoughtful friends that the awfulness of the Wassermans has little if anything to do with their being Jewish. She will, of course, agree. She is even heard to remark of recently met "quite attractive" Jews that they do not seem Jewish—meaning that they do not remind her of the Wassermans. For there in Barbara's mind is always the image of Mrs. Wasserman at the head of her table, her eyes wild and unfocused in that dreadful face, as she absorbs all the combined energies of her husband and her sons.

By the time Barbara and Martin see each other again, much has changed: terrible Mrs. Wasserman is dead, and Martin (as Martin Walters) has moved to San Francisco, and with his inheritance has bought a small and very smart antique store, and (what no one could conceivably have predicted) he is on the verge of a happy (if somewhat eccentric) marriage.

And so, at that time, once more he and Barbara fill spaces in each other's lives.

Four / 1951

A cold red February dusk, in the early fifties. On a suburban railway platform, south of San Francisco, two young women hurry toward each other. They are so unlike that their rush together seems improbable; one, Louisa, is very pregnant, stoop-shouldered, and rather shabby; the other girl, Kate, with dark red hair, is erect and stylish. But it is true; they are old friends who have not seen each other for five years, and not been truly in touch for longer than that.

"Oh, Louisa, you're beautiful pregnant!" Kate cries out.

Unused to kissing, and not quite used to shaking hands, they stand there grasping each other's arms.

"'Built-for-birth'—remember?" Ironically Louisa quotes the epithet from her early adolescence, "B.B.," which the standardized "popular" kids had repeated, tittering not quite out of her hearing, before she was discovered by Kate and became herself a popular Sub-Deb.

Even now Kate flushes. She was always popular (very), but she loved (and loves) her friend.

"And you're so chic!" Louisa says. (Is that a compliment?)

"Oh, well, I have to, with my silly job," says Kate, who works in the advertising department of a fashionable store. She is wearing a trim gray flannel coat, neat white gloves, high black patent shoes. She wears her hair long; she has long exotic dark eyes and an eager vulnerable mouth. A strong voluptuous body and an impetuous mind. She has been married for less than a year and her husband, a doctor, has been in Korea for the past five months. David: she often tries not to think of him at all, but this does not work.

The area around the small station has been fanatically landscaped: oleander bushes forced into smooth rounded shapes beside gently rising paths, and the parking lot is surrounded with smooth round stones that are gray in the dying light. The girls walk toward a large and muddy car, an old Hudson, with swollen sides—conspicuous among the bright new (postwar) station wagons and sparkling convertibles. "This is ours," says Louisa, and then, mysteriously, "Michael doesn't really *believe* in cars."

Kate has been told that Michael Wasserman is a graduate student, in psychology. She is a little afraid of this meeting; some of the intellectual awe in which she has always held Louisa has carried over to Michael—and it is worse since he is a man. (She really believes this.) Men usually like Kate, she bolsteringly reminds herself, but at the same time, she wishes that she had worn something else; she will feel overdressed in the pink silk that her coat now hides. (She is right—she will.) "Louisa," she says, "it's so marvelous to see you. I can't quite believe it. When does the baby come?"

"April. That's what I can't believe." Louisa laughs jerkily as, finally, the car starts up and they back vigorously out of the parking lot.

"I hope you'll have an absolutely beautiful girl who looks just like you."

This remark, although she knows it to be sincere (she knows Kate) makes Louisa stiffen; for one thing, she has never believed herself to be beautiful (though many people in her life have told and will tell her so); for another, she is passionately anxious that her child be a boy, so anxious that she has admitted this wish to no one. She mutters, "Christ, I'd drown her at birth," and she hunches down over the clutch, shifting violently.

"Oh, Louisa," chides Kate as she often did in the forties, ten years back, when Louisa's classically lovely face went unnoticed because her body was the wrong size: she was very tall, broad-hipped, with minuscule breasts. Shame made her gawky, and for a time the only boys who liked her were shrimps. (Were they trying to make her look worse, out there on the dance floor?)

"Well, at least I'll get to quit work next month," Louisa says. "I tell you—this job—in the Purchasing Department. Of course, I don't see how we'll manage. Even working Saturday mornings. Michael's parents—" she vaguely says.

None of this, besides a generalized sense of discontent (or fear?), makes much sense to Kate, but she decides to wait. She is looking forward to a drink. A martini, she hopes.

Between blocks of anonymous one-story California architecture, the old car heads toward a reddened sunset sky—heads west. The shade of the sky against the sharp black of the hills pierces Kate with nostalgia for those Virginia years of her late childhood, and she wants to say something to Louisa about what she still thinks of as home, but (out of character—she usually speaks her mind) she does not say this; she senses that Louisa is completely involved with her present life. Also, Louisa can be snappish; you have to be sure of her mood.

And so it is Louisa herself who asks, "Well, what do you hear from home?"

"Not much. You know Mother and Dad moved up to New Jersey a few years ago."

"No, I didn't."

"And I'm so terrible about writing. Only to David."

Quickly sympathetic (after all, it is her old friend Kate, not just a dangerous chic guest), Louisa asks, "David—how much longer will he be there, do you think?"

"Eighteen months, a year and a half."

"God, poor Kate."

"Well, yes. For one thing, he's so much fun to live with."

(She will not know how this sentence is to haunt her friend, or how Louisa is startled by it. Fun?)

"And he's so ambitious," Kate goes on heedlessly. "He really wants more surgical training. He's interested in hearts. And lungs."

"Oh" is what Louisa says, and then, "Some friends of ours are coming by after dinner, I think."

"You were so good to ask me down to dinner."

"Oh, it won't be much. Michael and I don't—" She lets whatever she meant to say trail off, and Kate suddenly understands that it is not so much that she is afraid of meeting Michael as she is afraid that he will be awful: a monstrous wasting of Louisa.

As he first appears, coming out to the car from the lamplit doorway of a small and literally vine-covered cottage, Michael is not terrible at all. He is short (well, of course; Kate was prepared for that), a little plump, blond, soft-fleshed, and very smiling. Jolly, he seems, in nice

Brooks Brothers clothes. (But why is he so much better dressed than Louisa is?)

He says, "I'm really glad you could come. Louisa's Southern Gothic childhood—of course she's mentioned you a lot."

He seems ebulliently eager to please—a quality that Kate finds sympathetic. She smiles, glad to like her old friend's husband.

The house is sparsely furnished with cheap-looking things that Kate supposes (rightly) to have come with the rental; a long dark lumpy sofa, some large and shapeless armchairs, a maple table and dining chairs. It is not very clean, tidy Kate discerns. (But she thinks: Who cares? What's really so important about cleaning a house?) It seems hastily pulled together, books and records stacked in corners—things shoved aside, or hidden.

Kate says, "God, what a marvelous smell! I never get enough garlic."

Louisa laughs with affection. "Kate, you sound so exactly like your*self*," she says.

Michael brings in a bottle of bourbon. "I'm afraid this is all we have," he beams.

"Marvelous—I'm dying for a drink." Kate doesn't like bourbon, but she thinks that perhaps this is just as well; she will drink less.

"You came down by *train*?" Michael asks, making it sound interesting. "How was it? We always drive, when we go. The Bayshore is my idea of what hell must look like —actualized."

"Of course we almost never hear from my parents," Louisa, who must have been thinking about this in the kitchen, comes in with glasses and ice and water.

Knowing Jack Calloway, Kate can well imagine: a handsome, charming, ultra-Southern man (though not from a very "good" family), who daily rides one of his mares, who talks well, telling stories with a flourish, and who loves parties and pretty ladies and strong drink. He is occasionally hospitalized for what are called nervous breakdowns, and is given electric shock, which calms him down. It has never been clear how he feels about his daughter, but Kate can too easily imagine how he would feel about Louisa's marriage. (Can that be partly why—Kate represses this half-formed question.)

"Even when I was so sick in Boston—I had colitis," Louisa says.

"They gave her cortisone, which precipitated a psychotic break. It happens fairly often," Michael gently explains.

"Jack never wrote. Caroline did, but such cold guilty letters—rather literary letters, actually. But at least I got the money for an analysis out of them. Not that it's doing any good."

"Now, honey—"

"And I hate those drives to the city."

Wholly confused, Kate merely notes that Louisa has taken to referring to her parents by their first names—to remove herself from them?

Michael laughs, but without much mirth. "It's hard to tell what's worse, the smothering attentions of my parents or the coldness of Louisa's. But of course smothering is exactly what they would like to do to Louisa. I think they had a great deal to do with her breakdown."

"Well, what are David's parents like?" Louisa asks, smiling but rather challenging.

"Uh, actually they're quite nice. They're divorced, but they've both remarried and the new marriages seem to be working out."

"Maybe that's the answer." Michael laughs again.

Louisa looks at him, stricken, so that he says, "Honey, of course I didn't mean us," and coming to stand behind her, pulling her back he kisses her.

Louisa's stomach is enormous. Kate tries (and fails) to imagine how that would be. A living child inside one? Instead she is struck with a pang of missing David, a pang that is vivid and sexual. "Louisa," she says quickly, "what about your work—do you still write poems and draw? Louisa is the most talented person I've ever known," Kate says, smiling to Michael.

"It's called 'too many minor talents.'" Louisa laughs, wry and self-deprecating. "No, I got tired of all that. Besides, I have so little time."

"But that's terrible—you did marvelous things."

"Marvelous for a thirteen-year-old, maybe. I'm afraid 'precocious' is the word." She frowns. "When I was crazy, I wrote a lot of poems. Poetry is Caroline, Caroline crying. I won't do that again."

Confused Kate tells her, "I still have the drawing you did of John."

"Really, you do?"

"Of course; it's a treasure. Every time I move, I'm careful to take it with me."

"I'll make more drinks," says Michael, and he does.

"I wonder where John is," Louisa says. "I think Caroline wrote that he married some fabulous New York beauty, an heiress or a model or something. John would marry someone mythic."

The two girls laugh, almost easily.

"The boy who broke my heart," Kate says. "God, how serious I was. But you know, that was a very bad thing for me. I did suffer."

"Really?" Louisa looks at her curiously. It is hard for her to believe that her attractive friend has been scarred—or perhaps she is too concentrated on her own scarring. Looking at Michael, she says that she had better see about dinner.

The quality of their connection, Michael's with Louisa, is still quite obscure to Kate. She sees only that it is very unlike hers with David, and she thinks: David and I are noisier and more open, but then Louisa has always been more complicated than I am. She has a dim sense that Michael is controlling Louisa in some subtle way, although on the surface he is agreeable, somewhat passive.

They have dinner on the square maple table. Michael eats ravenously, breaking and buttering his bread while Louisa serves the coq au vin, and rice.

"Louisa, how marvelous this is," Kate says. "And the rice!"

"I have some sort of atavistic thing with rice," Louisa says.

"My mother is an appalling cook," says Michael, "but she's somehow perpetrated a myth that she's terrific. God, the years of dry roast chicken and overdone beef, and everyone sitting around saying how great it is."

This speech makes Kate uncomfortable; she is not sure why. She says, "I like to cook," hoping for a change of subject. And she adds, "I'm not terribly good—yet."

But Michael goes on. "And she sends me clothes, embarrassing big packages from Brooks. God! My brother still lives at home—of course he's gay."

This is an unfamiliar word to Kate, but she senses what he must mean, and does not want to hear about it. She turns to Louisa, and speaks in her old forthright way. "But I think you should go on doing those things you used to do. You were good—everyone thought so, and I know you were."

"Louisa is very ambivalent about what might be intellectual competition." Michael explains. "She's afraid I might slap her down, the way her father always did. Isn't that true, honey?"

Louisa sounds tired. "I suppose so," she says. "Or afraid I wouldn't do anything really good. I think it's more that."

A terrible sense of strangeness suddenly overwhelms Kate; what is she doing there with those two people? She feels lonely, lost, with her old friend who has become a mumbling stranger. (Louisa is still in some way very sick. Miserable. Her eyes are desperate.) Why are she and Louisa here at all, thousands of miles from home? Why this husband, this Michael, whose heavy presence dominates the room?

But then the doorbell rings, and Michael gets up to let other people in.

A couple, young and good-looking, obviously "Eastern" in their style. Kate is at least momentarily reassured; she sees these people as landmarks. Sally and Andrew Chapin. Sally is hugely pregnant with their third child. Andrew is a graduate student in English; he has just got a new book by Lionel Trilling, which has several essays on Freud, on psychoanalysis, and he wonders what Michael thinks about it.

Michael hasn't seen the Trilling book, but he says what he imagines it will be like; he uses words like "eclectic" and "neo-"(attached to a variety of names). Andrew and Louisa both listen to this as though it were extraordinary stuff, and for all Kate knows it is.

But then, as she listens (or half listens) to the two men, a sort of bell sounds in Kate's mind, and she repeats the name: "Andrew Chapin?"

Interrupted, they both turn to her—both with (dissimilar) slight frowns.

Andrew says, "You're thinking of my father. A writer. He was very popular for a while. A brief career, poor guy," he adds.

"Oh, of course. My mother was mad for him."

"He was an unusual talent," Michael announces, frowning more intensely and giving Kate the impression that he would prefer not to share the talents of "Andrew Chapin" with Kate's mother. (Poor Jane Flickinger: Kate smiles involuntarily at this summoning of her mother, for whom she feels a kind of tolerant affection.)

Michael is, in fact, fascinated by the elder Andrew Chapin (who wrote delicately of exacerbated New England consciences, who hinted at wild sexual distortions; it was Martin who first gave Michael those books). And Michael is impressed with knowing the writer's son—as Andrew is fascinated by Michael. And given the perversity of human attractions it is perhaps not odd that they are drawn to qualities in the other that each man himself could have done without: a famous father, Jewishness. Andrew also envies Michael's laziness (he castigates his own compulsive habits of work); Michael's unbridled appetite (Andrew has ulcers and a generally difficult stomach).

Much later in life Louisa is to decide that to love Michael is to hate oneself.

Andrew is a trim dark boy, with interesting heavy eyebrows, who reminds Kate very slightly of David, except that David's face is witty, wry, whereas this boy is very serious. (In fact he is desperate: he wants to write, to be a writer, and he cannot write.) He is also very rich; the first Andrew invested his meteoric twenties' earnings very astutely. Sally, his wife, is a small neat blonde, with soft peach fuzz on her chin (later to bristle), who "adores" her husband. She is a bright girl in her own right, but she is brainwashed by currently popular ideas about the functions of wives.

Also, her own parents divorced and frequently remarried —she won't do that (she is only to marry twice).

Kate has just been struck with an idea—or, rather, a perception so startling that she thinks she must be drunk, although she knows that she is not: looking at Michael, at his broad Slavic brow and arrogant nose, she sees that beneath his soft flesh and fair hair is the skull of Jack Calloway. Not that they look alike—Jack's skin is florid and his hair quite dark—but the bones are the same. What can this mean? Has Louisa noticed? Why didn't someone stop this marriage?

Michael has gone back to lecturing Andrew on Trilling. "Also," he winds up, "I always thought that story of his—what was the name? Time or something."

"'Of This Time, Of That Place,'" Kate surprisingly (to Michael) fills in for him. It happens to be a favorite story of hers.

"Yes, I think you're right," Michael says. "Anyway, I always thought it was a very homosexual story."

"What on earth do you mean by that?" Kate bursts out. "I don't think you mean anything at all." She hopes that this is the worst that she is going to say, and fears that it is not.

Michael takes on a patient tone. "Naturally I don't mean literally homosexual, but the central concern is with relationships between men. One might in the same way say that Hemingway is a homosexual writer."

"God," says Kate, who is beginning to feel that she has had more than she can stand. This is the intellectual world? She repeats, "I don't think you mean anything at all."

Michael is enjoying this exchange. Attracted to Kate, and very self-absorbed, he has a poor sense of audience—of how he is coming across. He believes that Kate is enjoying the conversation, too (or that she should). He says, "I mean homosexual in the sense that I might describe your relationship with Louisa as homosexual, in that it was most intense in your prepuberty days, wasn't it? A sort or preadolescent love affair."

"No!" Kate cries out, meaning no to everything he says.

At last Michael understands that she is irritated, and he does not help by saying, "I think you're being a little literal."

"*I'm* literal! You're the literal one! You've got to put the same label on everything."

Louisa has risen and is clearing the table. She looks very uncomfortable. Kate makes a gesture to help, but she is refused, and she is then spurred on by the sight of her pregnant friend bearing piles of dirty dishes.

"And why does Louisa have to work in a purchasing department? Why aren't you working and letting her get a degree in something? I'm sure she'd rather."

"You don't see a difference in roles?" Michael asks, again warming to the discussion. "I prefer the tension between opposites. Louisa's femaleness makes me feel more male. You don't believe in sexual polarity?"

"No, I don't think so," says Kate, and for the first time she begins to be aware of what she does think, and in her enthusiasm about a new idea her anger at Michael somewhat diminishes. "I believe in a man and a woman living together, being friends. I don't think it matters who does what. David is a better cook than I am. While he was interning and I was working, we sort of cooked together—it was fun. I don't think it matters who does dishes or stays at home with kids."

"Well, you would have made an awfully pretty suffragette," says Andrew, laughing. And he has succeeded in lightening the moment (not only because he is a nice man; he is also strongly attracted to Kate).

Kate blushes, both for the compliment and for what she has said. "But I mean it," she says, purposely exaggerating her forthrightness—this is a way she has.

Sally Chapin looks incredulously at Kate; she can hardly believe that such a pretty and well-dressed girl could have such—such ideas. And her vocabulary comes up with no word to describe Kate's point of view. "Masculine" is the word most generally used (at that time) to describe unfortunate behavior in women, but that does not seem quite appropriate.

"Kate, I really don't think you've given this much thought," Louisa says.

"No, I haven't," says honest Kate, "but you know how I am. Instinctual."

"Well, Michael thinks all the time. He's extremely intellectual." Louisa feels the old thrill of defending Michael: there was a triumphant moment, some years ago at Michael's parents' house, when Louisa told his mother *please* to stop interrupting what Michael was saying.

Kate then says, "Oh, God, my train! I have to go!"

Andrew, who has just become conscious of how attracted he is, and who for the first time is a little irritated by Michael, asks, "Can't we take you to your train? We have to go, too. Louisa, Michael—okay?"

Louisa agrees, and so, because of the rush, the farewells are minimized, and what might have been somewhat awkward is capsuled.

"Goodbye—great to see you—thanks!"

Everyone says these things, and then Louisa and Michael are left alone.

This is often a bad moment for them, but the evening has produced a mood of affectionate rapport. They have, at times, almost the quality of a conspiracy, an alliance against all other people, which other people sometimes sense (Sally Chapin does) and find unpleasant.

"God, she's really got much worse," Louisa says. "She used to be sort of marvelous."

"Really? She did? I got a strong sense that there's something terribly wrong with her marriage, didn't you?" poor Michael says eagerly. "She seemed so defensive, as though she were projecting."

"I'm sure you're right. He's probably some real jerk, and she's sorry she married him."

"Do you ever get the feeling that Andrew Chapin is essentially boring?"

"Well, yes, and God knows Sally is."

"*Yes*. Well, time for bed?" he says, smiling.

"I think I'm frustrated, that's what's wrong with me," laughs Kate, somewhat embarrassed, as she settles into the Chapins' car. "I really didn't mean to be so disagreeable."

"You really weren't," says gentlemanly Andrew, who is kind.

"Michael can be awfully—psychological," Sally says softly. She has just realized with a start that she doesn't like Michael at all. (In fact—it is years before she knows this —Sally likes very few people.) And she thinks this violent "different" girl is interesting.

"Well, it is his field," Andrew reminds her, out of a feeling that someone should stand up for Michael.

At the station, where they are just in time—the train is coming up from the South (southern California)—Kate thanks them in her enthusiastic way. She says, "Please call me when you come up to the city. David Harrington." She says this proudly; she likes David's name, likes wearing it. "I'd love to see you."

But by the time they do call her, or, rather, Andrew does, she is not at first quite sure who he is.

Five / 1955

From birth, Maude Wasserman, the daughter of Louisa and Michael, has been a startling child. She refused to be breast-fed (which did not help Louisa's own feelings about her breasts); she would not go to sleep without music playing in her room. By the time she was one, she had begun to talk, and she wanted to be read to all the time; she demanded new Little Golden Books on every trip to the market. She memorized her favorites, *Crispin's Crispian* ("Crispin was a dog who belonged to himself . . .") and *The Sailor Dog* ("Born in the teeth of a gale, Scupper was a sailor . . ."). But at two she still did not walk. Michael, who had great faith in tests, had her tested with every available battery of psychological-neurological-muscular tests, all of which revealed nothing, except that she was unusually bright. She was a remarkably fast crawler. She had a great many inexplicable and alarming chest infections. She was very blond. (Louisa's hair by now had darkened to a blacky brown.)

On the Easter Sunday in April which is a month before Maude is to be three, she is as tall as a five-year-old, and she almost knows how to read.

"I don't want to wear the blue," she screams at Louisa, reddening dangerously. "I won't go!"

They are invited to an Easter-egg hunt at the Chapins' house, which is next door. After Maude was born, and despite a lot of discussion about the inadvisability of living next door to close friends, Louisa and Michael moved next to Andrew and Sally; it was as though they could not bear to be alone, once isolated with a baby (or so Louisa later thinks of that move).

"I want to wear the pink!" Maude screams.

The pink dress is almost outgrown; it makes Maude look too tall. Weedish, neglected.

Nearly sick with indecision (these small crises are more than she can stand), Louisa yields, but she says, "Are you sure you don't want to wear the blue? It's new."

And then (startlingly) Maude changes her mind. "The blue! I don't want to wear the pink—it's babyish!"

(An uncomforting victory.)

Louisa herself is wearing pale green. It is a new dress, a present from her mother, from Caroline in Virginia, and perhaps for that reason (she has never really trusted Caroline) Louisa is unsure of the color—of how she looks.

As they say goodbye to each other, Louisa and Michael avoid each other's eyes, and they no longer kiss —ever. Michael says, "Honey, have a good time!" to both of them, and Louisa grasps her daughter's hand.

A familiar but never quite named panic fills her chest, and she holds Maude's hand hard. (Does Maude feel it, too, her mother's terror, wherever she goes?)

The two houses are separated by a rough seven-foot redwood fence which was erected by Louisa and Michael's landlady, Mrs. Cornwallis, who is a small and violent woman, probably insane. (They put up a political poster, cut and rearranged to spell "Nix—on—Ike," and she telephoned: "You get that thing down! Get it down! I won't have my house defaced." Well, it was her house, wasn't it? Michael says this; and sick, though separately so, they take it down.) Their house—Mrs. Cornwallis's house—is redwood, like the fence; it is a cube, new and raw, and the lawn is also new, not doing well. The rent takes exactly half their income from Michael's instructor job.

The Chapins' house is their own, the down payment a present from generous parents. It is five years old, an old house for that neighborhood, in California. It is white, and a small vined porch gives it a friendly look.

As Louisa and Maude go down the front path to the driveway, down the driveway to the sidewalk, festive smells and sounds drift over the high fence: smoke, and the swish of a garden hose, ice in glasses, flowers and new-mown grass. Spring earth—it is Easter Sunday.

There are two cars in the Chapins' driveway: their new Ford station wagon (blue) and an old (1946) Chrysler convertible, with real wood. In perfect condition. It is the Magowans' car—dazzling and splendid friends of the Chapins, with three marvelous children. Douglas, Allison, and Jennifer.

Of course they would be there, Louisa had known that; still, their wonderful car further lowers her heart.

As they approach the house—Louisa and Maude, clutching hands—Andrew comes around a corner, dark Andrew, barefoot, in jeans and a white T-shirt, carrying the hose. He grins a crooked welcome. "What pretty ladies! Say, Lou, that dress matches your eyes."

And in that sunstruck instant all Louisa's dread dissolves. Her blood warms, and she looks at Andrew, her kind old familiar friend, and she thinks: Of course, I am in love with Andrew.

Her heart in her eyes, she only says, "Michael had to work on his thesis." She begins to laugh, somewhat hysterically. "He hates Easter parties."

Andrew laughs, too; they share an interest in Michael's Jewishness. It still seems a little exotic to them both. Michael and Andrew (and Louisa) are agreed that the best American writers (now) are either Southern or Jewish, which holds out no hope for poor Andrew—but as they see it, Maude can't miss, with her dual heritage. (And curiously enough this prophecy or wish turns out remarkably to be true: at an early age Maude begins to write, and she goes on.)

Maude is smiling; she has always liked Andrew.

The three of them go around the side of the house, with Maude in front, then Andrew, then Louisa. Andrew holds back a branch of shrubbery for Louisa, and their hands meet briefly. Electric! He smiles at her, and she is incredibly happy.

All the Magowans are blond—large blond people, three large blond children, and Alex and Grace. Since Sally Chapin is also fair, as are her children, and Maude, the yard seems full of blondness—yellow hair all over, like patches of sunshine. This lightness of complexion is one of the things that ordinarily alienate Louisa—making her feel dark, a stranger. But today she looks at Andrew, who is darker than she, and terribly familiar. (In fact, he looks like someone from the depths of her life, but who?)

An uneasy hostess, Sally does not come forward to greet Louisa and Maude: well, after all, they live next door; she sees them every day. But even the most welcome guests (she is crazy about the Magowans; Alex and Grace are the most terrific people)—any guests at all—make Sally feel invaded; her tight family group is easily threatened. Now she unenthusiastically says "Hi" to Louisa, and, more warmly (children are easier for her), "Maudie, you're so pretty in that blue."

"Hi, Louisa, great to see you. Old Michael hitting the books?" This is the language of the Magowans, both of them.

"Yes, still on his thesis."

They are relieved that Michael has not come. Sensing this, though dimly, Louisa feels a rare instant of affection for her husband: poor Michael, who makes so many people uncomfortable, and never knows.

Normally shy and hesitant, Maude runs off to a corner of the garden where the other children have clustered. Looking after her, Louisa is struck (as she is repeatedly, *still*) at the oddity of her, Louisa, having a blond daughter. Despite the fact that Michael is blond, and that she herself was a blond little girl, before it all went dark. In fact today, this Easter, all those seven children—three Magowans, three Chapins, one Wasserman—might be themselves a family, an interrelated California tribe.

"Lou, what'll you have to drink?" Andrew has put out some bottles and a bowl of ice under a trellis of wisteria that he finished last weekend. Louisa has noticed this: the Chapins work at the quality of their life, at improving it; they make large and small efforts at having a better time together, whereas she and Michael make none at all. (But if they did?)

"A gin? Gin and tonic?"

"Great. How do you feel about limes?"

"I'm mad for limes." She laughs.

"Terrific."

He hands her a tall cold glass and they exchange a look—does he feel it, too?

Then Louisa goes over to sit on the grass with Sally and Alex and Grace.

It is a marvelous balmy April day. The softly petaled fruit trees are in bloom at the end of the garden, and Sally's thick sweet peas, all lovely pastel shades, climb with their tiny tentacles to almost cover the Chapin side of the fence. In the back of this row of houses—the Chapins', Mrs. Cornwallis's—the tawny California hills lie sloping gently under the sun, here and there darkened with the shadow of a cloud, and darkly patched at intervals with live oaks, spreading green. (Hills that within the next few years are to be raped by subdivisions.)

The other families on that street where the Wassermans and Chapins live have more money (much) than Michael and Louisa do, but they are uneducated people, white-collar workers, whose houses and whose children are kept immaculate, the children not allowed to run naked through hoses in the summer, children sent to Sunday School on Sundays. Although she knows better (she thinks), Louisa is made uncomfortable by those people, those Ike-supporters who are later to be called Middle Americans —she is made to feel that she is a disgrace. Thank God the Chapins are there—but somehow they are less disgraceful than she is.

The Magowan children, though uniformly blond, are otherwise remarkably unlike. Douglas, the oldest, is tall and erect, and an absolutely fearless child: no swing too high for him, no dog too large. Allison, the middle child, is so far the "difficult" one. Nervous and a little shy, much too thin, with scabbed knees, today she runs over from the other children to cling to her mother's arm.

"Mommy, I don't feel like hiding eggs." The children have all been given baskets of eggs to hide; later in the afternoon, in theory, they will all go hunting for the ones the others hid.

"Darling, please don't whine. I can't stand the sound."

She says it so pleasantly, and yet with such certainty. Grace knows her own mind. And Louisa hopelessly envies that confident, smooth motherhood. Maude's whines affect her own stomach, so that she tends to respond angrily; Maude's tantrums make her physically sick. But today Maude is fine. (Why?)

Jennifer, the youngest Magowan, is placid and plump. (And she is to remain so, despite family disasters and her own troubled first love affair.)

"But I don't know where to put any eggs!" Allison complains.

Grace laughs. "You don't? Not in the whole big garden?" Then she whispers, but so that they all can hear: "I bet you never thought of a high-up place. You see those plum trees? Where the branches spread out?"

And Allison runs off.

No wonder Sally Chapin admires Grace so much. ("She's really the neatest girl.") Grace can do anything, and does: she bakes all their bread, plus cakes and pies and cookies; she upholsters furniture—marvelous junk that she and Alex have refinished themselves; she makes all the clothes that her daughters wear, and sometimes shirts for Alex and Douglas. She also plays the piano, a funny sort of honky-tonk that she picked up somewhere in her New Hampshire girlhood, and she is very good at charades. Today she is wearing a yellow halter dress, exhibiting terrific breasts. It is true that Grace has everything.

But today Louisa doesn't really mind. She is in love with Andrew, and it seems just barely possible that he might love her, or perhaps sometime kiss her: at a party they could go out together for more ice, or hot dogs. Something.

And, looking over at Andrew, Louisa is suddenly struck, so that she cries out, "Andrew, it's just come to me: you look so much like a boy I grew up with. John Jeffreys."

Sally laughs a little; she looks curiously at Louisa. "Some old boyfriend out of your Southern past?"

"Well, no." She laughs. "I should have been so lucky." (She has picked up a lot of Yiddishisms from Michael, which, characteristically, she overdoes.) "Every girl in town was crazy about John." This last is said directly to Andrew: "I am crazy about you" is in her eyes. "In fact he broke my best friend's heart."

"Oh, he sounds terrible," Sally says.

And Alex Magowan. "Bad news, from the sound of it." He chuckles.

Andrew is interested. "Your best friend? You mean that girl we met at your house a few years ago? With dark red hair?"

(Andrew was disturbingly attracted to Kate, so much so that he called her once when he had gone up to San Francisco to get a new suit at Brooks. He asked her to have lunch with him, telling himself that that was all he meant, but it somehow got out of hand: he had made what they both knew was a pass.)

Louisa is astonished. "Kate—you met Kate?" And then she remembers. "Oh, of course, four years ago. Sally and I were both pregnant."

"She was awfully attractive," Sally says (doubtfully). "Whatever happened to her—did her husband get back from Korea? I remember she told us she was 'frustrated.' " Sally giggles at this boldness.

"We've sort of lost touch," Louisa admits. Then she says, "It's terrible, I'll call her tomorrow." And she believes that she will do this.

The truth is she has been too depressed, and unwilling for Kate to see her in still another furnished house, Michael with a still-unfinished degree, and a baby who cries so much, who is so often sick.

Then, suddenly, all the children begin to scream at once.

"Mother, look at Douglas!"

"Look, there's Douglas on the fence!"

"Hey, Mom, look at me!"

All the grownups look, and there, unbelievably, is small Douglas against the April sky; he is standing on top of the fence, balanced there.

None of them knows what to do. Then Alex springs up and heads toward his son. "Stay there, old man. I'll help you down."

But with a wild pirate's grin Douglas has leapt down, to fall on the spring earth as softly as a bird might plummet down—to fall in a heap from which he quickly arises, dirty and triumphant. Alex reaches the boy; he grasps him, picks him up under the arms, and holds him out in the air (but not as high as Douglas by himself just was); Alex is quietly domineering, saying, "Look, that was a pretty dangerous thing to do."

Grace laughs permissively, although for a moment she makes a gesture of clutching at her throat. (Is that where her anxiety lives? Louisa's is in her gut.) "You know, everyone says it's terrific to have such a fearless child," says Grace. "But I can tell you—sometimes—" and she laughs again. Her long hair is caught up in a smooth low knot, and she now pushes back a stray lock.

"Well, how about lunch?" says Sally, and she and Louisa go into the cozy Chapin kitchen to bring things out. Often, both Louisa and Michael make Sally nervous; they are so intelligent, so Eastern, so critical. They and Andrew talk so much. (Andrew who is also Eastern and intelligent. And critical.)

But today Sally and Louisa are in a mood of warmer rapport than usual.

"Having the Magowans over always makes me a little nervous," Sally confides. "You know, she's such a fantastic cook, and everything."

"Well, you're awfully good. That's how I sometimes feel about you—nervous," Louisa says, and they both laugh wildly at that, because it is less than half true.

Louisa's cooking is as erratic as everything else about her at this time. Often barely able to get a mediocre meal on the table, she occasionally emerges to near greatness: a truly superb single dish; less frequently, a great dinner. Once, after too many martinis, she underdid a pot roast in the pressure cooker, and produced a roast that was marvelously tender and succulent.

Now Sally says, "Remember your pot roast? Andrew still talks about that."

Louisa laughs. "So does Michael." (What Michael says is "That time you got drunk and we had the good pot roast.")

They have cold sliced ham and potato salad and garlic bread and corn on the cob and cold fried chicken. Sally's menus tend to be a little odd. For dessert there is chocolate ice cream and strawberries.

The children eat on an old plaid steamer rug (from Andrew's parents) at the end of the garden, the grownups at the table beneath the wisteria trellis. From time to time Louisa glances over to where Maude sits among the others, half expecting her to be doing something terrible—hitting, pulling someone's hair—and to feel her own stomach clutch with panic, as though it were she who had struck out at the world. But Maude is fine; today she is an attractive child, in a group of attractive children.

As, today, Louisa is an attractive woman. Sometimes with the Chapins, especially Sally (or worse, Grace Magowan), she has felt a dark alienation, an impossible division: she is not a woman (her breasts are too small). Dutifully she says the same things that the other women say; she speaks with affection of Michael, with tender love of Maude. And sometimes she believes what she is saying. (It does not occur to her that other women could also be acting out parts.)

Alex Magowan is a generally pleasant but silent young man, an engineer who will eventually become extremely successful. (Indeed, he will change the skyline of San Francisco.) Aside from an occasional small comment, these days he appears to have very little to say to anyone but Grace. As a couple, they project extraordinary self-sufficiency (which makes their later history all the more remarkable).

Now he addresses Louisa, rather formally. "Louisa, I really wanted to talk to you. Grace and I have a sort of —uh—proposition to make to you."

Looking at Andrew, Louisa laughs. "Well, God knows I'm open to propositions." (As though this were untrue.)

"Sally showed us some of the sketches you made of her kids—"

Sally: "I hope you won't mind, Lou."

"And Grace and I were wondering if maybe you could do something with our group."

Grace: "Of course, we want to *pay* you."

Alex: "You could think about it."

"Well, that's really nice of you." Louisa is so pleased that she doesn't know how to respond. "They're great looking kids," she flounders.

"Nothing fancy, like a portrait," Alex says. "Just sketches. You think about it and let us know. About the money."

"Well, I've never really been paid, I wouldn't know—any idea—" But she is already thinking greedily: Enough money for a new dress, black, for Andrew to see her in, the next time there's a party? Or maybe some velvet pants.

"You have to charge for what you do," says Grace decisively.

Elation makes Louisa's mind whirl about, directionless. She is thinking that Andrew isn't actually like John Jeffreys at all. Andrew is Eastern, Northeastern; there are Atlantic generations behind him. Seaboard summers of sun and fine blown sand, billowing waves and sand dunes, have set the tone of his voice and the lights in his eyes. Whereas John's summers were as Southern as Louisa's own: wide muddy rivers hung with moss, turgid honeysuckle caves and dim sweet flowering shrubs beside country roads at night, where young lovers stop to kiss. And that is what Louisa wants with Andrew: just to kiss, their mouths to meet, their arms to hold each other, as sweetly as she and Richard used to kiss. Not sex: not the terrible naked writhings that she and Michael go through, the harsh mechanical touching, the nervous hot embarrassment. Not that. Just kissing.

"You'd better let me be your agent," Andrew says. "I can see you don't have much of a head for business."

Has he understood? What message has he caught from her? Louisa's heart is as light as a bird.

"Well, honey," Michael says, "I'm just not sure." His voice is high and tight, a constipated voice, which by now has a physical effect on Louisa: she experiences a familiar pain in her lower intestine, along with a sodden weight in her heart.

"I don't know," Michael continues—he has no notion of his effect on Louisa. "It just seems a funny sort of offer to make to someone as talented as you are. I mean, commercial art—and portraiture is pretty commercial, isn't it? —commercial art just isn't your *thing*."

"I don't want any supper," says Maude.

What would Grace Magowan do with a child who said that? Insist, or let it go? Either way, she would instantly know (Louisa imagines); she would do just the right thing. Torn, not knowing anything, Louisa compromises. "Couldn't you try?"

"Now, Maudie," says her father, who has been eating as he talked, "your mother says to try."

"No!" She bursts into tears.

Which is what Louisa would like to do. Instead she says furiously, "In that case you leave the table! You go to your room!"

For several minutes the two adults (are they that?) sit trapped in the sounds of their daughter's diminishing sobs.

Then Michael says, "I'll finish the meat loaf," and he helps himself.

Louisa lights a cigarette.

Is Michael an appalling person, whom Louisa should rightfully despise? No, and as yet she does not despise him, nor has she any idea of the crippling extent of her own misery, the devastating depression she is in (and that he is in). She doesn't dare think about it because (she is sure) there is no way out.

They have no money. Both are children of rich and successful fathers who fear that indulgence will "spoil" them, those two wounded and literally spoiled offspring. (This is the one area of agreement between Jack Calloway and Saul Wasserman.) Sometimes a parental check will come, which immediately goes for either bills or a blowout, an expensive and often unenjoyed restaurant meal—"But we haven't been out for so long." They say of themselves that they are broke (it sounds better); the truth is that they are poor.

Or, if not poor, they are economically lower middle class, and they suffer some of the injustices and indignities of that group. Since they did not have enough cash (around a hundred dollars) for a refrigerator, they had to buy one on time—thus, with interest, paying around two hundred. And, having discovered the forbidden delights of time payments, they are also buying a vacuum cleaner and a sewing machine. The garbage collector stops their account, and they have to take their own big rusty cans to the dump. Their lack of money is a constant presence, a weight on their spirits.

Louisa is terrified of her own despair. Michael is afraid of his parents. He married Louisa, having mistaken hysteria for strength; she would protect him. But now he is afraid of her, too, and she is no protection at all. His professors are horrendous and irrational giants, to be laboriously placated. With Mrs. Cornwallis, the local enemy, he is apologetic, which increases Louisa's panic.

The evening now looms ahead of them.

"I have a sort of stomach ache," Louisa says. "I think I'll lie down for a while."

"Okay. I have to work."

"I'll clear up later."

"I'll check on Maude," he says.

And so with small promises they separate.

In their bedroom Louisa lies across the bed. She hears Michael reading to Maude. (He loves to read aloud.) He reads for a long time, half an hour or so, and then Louisa hears him leave Maude's room (quietly; she must be asleep, thank God) and go into the bathroom. To avoid the sounds he makes there (he spends hours in the bathroom), she quickly gets up and goes into the kitchen, where inefficiently she does most of the dishes; she is never quite able to finish them all.

Michael comes into the kitchen. "Honey, can I read you something?"

Drying her greasy hands on a damp towel, she turns to face him.

"In effect, the dichotomy between—"

He goes on, but Louisa has stopped hearing. She is thinking about Andrew: his bare brown feet with strong tendons, long toes with a few black hairs on them. His amused, perked-up thick eyebrows. She thinks: I long to kiss him.

"So what do you think?" asks Michael.

"It's really good. It's—uh—*terse*, isn't it?"

He likes the word. "Terse. Yes. Very. Not a wasted word. That's why it takes me so long. But what do you think? Maybe it should be expanded. Maybe even a few *dull* patches?"

"No, I don't think so."

This is as close to communicating as they come, these days.

Later Louisa will get into bed with a pile of paperback

mysteries (limp, thumbed volumes: she forgets and some-times reads them several times). By the time Michael comes to bed, she will be pretending to be asleep.

When did they enjoy love together? Louisa can hardly remember, but with an effort she recalls lunches urgently pushed aside in a rush toward bed, in those early married months. In the terrible Boston attic. More recently (and more clearly) she sees herself reaching, touching his warm soft flesh, and she hears his sympathetic voice: "Do you feel very sexy, honey?"

And the frantic doomed attempts they make. Michael thinks that he is impotent; she thinks that she is frigid. At this stage neither blames the other.

In fact neither of these intelligent hyper-educated people has any idea of the extent to which they are damaging to each other. Michael is now as afraid of Louisa as he used to be of his parents—she is both parents. No wonder his asthma is worse; no wonder he is impotent.

Louisa still sees her psychiatrist twice a month. Dr. Chernoff. And sometimes, in moods of strength, she says that she thinks she should leave Michael. They should di-vorce.

Chernoff, who is a shy, kindly, and unimaginative man, thinks not. The idea seems to upset him (but of course this is not true; psychiatrists do not become upset). In fact at moments Louisa imagines that Chernoff identifies with Michael, that they are somehow linked—two intelligent and kindly Jewish men against an evil gentile.

But she does not trust her (accurate) perceptions of Dr. Chernoff, and he is another reason for not leaving Michael.

A few weeks later (and as though by telepathy), Caroline sends Louisa a pair of black velvet pants, with a note that sounds apologetic.

Louisa and Michael believe that Caroline is apologizing for a gesture that could be construed as "spoiling." ("She has identified with your father," Michael explains. "Incorporated.") But actually there is a terrible failure of understanding between Caroline and her daughter: the truth is that Caroline, as though with a mysterious foreknowledge of a relatively early death, is obsessively devoting her efforts (involving secret sessions with lawyers) to a trust fund for Louisa, one untouchable by Jack Calloway—who, with some reason, Caroline does not count on for justice. Thus Caroline does not often send money to Louisa, and she feels that she must apologize for presents. (A misunderstanding indeed, and sad: but eventually that trust is one of the things that is to save Louisa.)

In the meantime, wearing her new pants to a party, getting very drunk, Louisa tells Andrew Chapin that she is in love with him.

A dance, in fact. One of the graduate students is house-sitting in the expensive fake-adobe of one of the more successful professors (from the Education Department). The host provides the space, and a stack of records (a sentimental fellow; his collection specializes in the forties). Guests bring their own bottles, which is an arrangement that does not work out very well: those who brought "dago red" are seen drinking the "good Scotch" of others—and besides people are getting drunk in uneven, disparate ways.

Louisa is getting drunk on the Scotch that Andrew brought and pours for her, although she has never liked Scotch. The nostalgic music (Glen Miller, T. Dorsey, Benny Goodman) reminds her of her early adolescence, those Tin Can dances, and Richard (and Kate, and John Jeffreys). Drunkenly she sees it all as beautiful, as golden, and she clings to Andrew as they dance—she is in love!

They go out onto the patio for air; they walk slowly toward a huge concealing clump of shrubbery. Abruptly they stop—they kiss.

Their bodies grind together, and their mouths—they grasp and reach. They come apart, and Louisa is first to speak. "Andrew, couldn't we go somewhere in your car—to get ice—anything?"

"Louisa, I wouldn't dare." He is just sober enough to tell the truth. The notion of extramarital love is as frightening to Andrew as anarchy would be (where would it end?); he is both orderly and ambivalent.

"But, Andrew, I love you. I have for months—"

"Now, Lou," he admonishes her. And he tries to joke: "I don't want you to hate me in the morning."

"I love you!"

(Love?)

But as she understands what he has said, and that he meant it, she is overwhelmed by a violent wave of nausea.

She is wretchedly sick, and hung over the next day. And miserably embarrassed.

The memory of that evening becomes a source of acute discomfort, mingled with the taste of bile. ("Andrew, I love you—" How could she have said it?)

For days and weeks after that, she and Andrew avoid each other, he out of a shy inability to tell her that, after all, they are friends (or, better, to tell her he's changed his mind, to take her to a motel on El Camino Real, on the way up to San Francisco: he gives that a lot of thought). And Louisa avoids him out of shame. So at last they both (incorrectly) assume disapproval on the other's part.

Six / 1958

The scalloped neckline of Louisa's flowered taffeta dress is coyly designed to half reveal breasts; Louisa fumbles at it, her fingers pleat the gaps. She has come to have lunch with Kate, in Kate's sprawling Victorian flat on Potrero Hill. Taffeta—at lunch, on Potrero Hill? She must have been crazy (she must be crazy).

The dress was a present from Mrs. Wasserman, who occasionally goes rushing through Filene's Basement propelled by some curious grab bag of emotions toward Louisa —possibly guilt, less probably generosity. The result is a large box of clothes: dresses, sweaters, once a coat (but a size 8, not much help, and of course these bargains cannot be returned, even if Louisa dared complain). Louisa writes letters of profuse thanks (her ineradicable Southern training, from Caroline) and she wears the clothes. For all she knows, they are terrific, and becoming to her. So faulty at this time is her own sense of herself that she has no idea what she looks like, much less what she should wear.

Kate is wearing a blue denim skirt (a wraparound

—she is four months pregnant), a pink oxford-cloth shirt, small pink scarf. She looks wonderful; she always does. "Louisa, you're so dressed up, " she has inevitably said. But added, "Your hair looks marvelous. I love it long."

(Her hair?)

This long-planned and often postponed visit (Louisa and Michael have been living in San Francisco, "The City," for a couple of years now) is not going terribly well. Kate's second child, a little girl, is at home with a cold, which makes her cross, and demanding of her mother—so much so that Kate, the affectionate friend, is divided. And this pregnancy is more difficult than the other two: Kate feels queasy a lot of the time, and she worries about the baby (who will be a beautiful blond girl, to be named Louisa).

Louisa keeps eying the phone. She has to call someone, a man named Dan, to say that she can meet him this afternoon. (Kate will be her excuse.) But Dan drives a cab; he is almost never at home—when should she call? Also it is not entirely certain that he will want to see her. (It never is—she must be crazy.)

Kate's flat has a look that Louisa finds striking, and that she cannot at first define, but then it comes to her that the rooms look like Kate herself: Louisa could almost have come in and named this place as Kate's. Vigorous and forthright colors, dark greens in the living room with a little orange, a lot of white. A bowl of daisies, a vase of dark green leaves. A bedroom of red and pink. (A sexy room: if she had a room like that, for love, would Dan be in love with her? She doubts it.)

"I have to make a phone call," Louisa says.

"It's right there. How about a Bloody Mary? I think we ought to celebrate. I haven't seen you forever!"

"Swell."

Dan is not at home.

The little girl comes into the room sniffling. She is a redhead, like Kate and like her brother Stephen. ("It's really embarrassing," Kate has said. "Like those dumb ads about never underestimating a woman's power, or something.")

"Mommy, I want you to read to me."

"Darling, I can't. You see I have company."

"But I want you to read!"

"Darling, I've told you, I can't read right now. Louisa and I are talking."

Maude by now would have been screaming, and Louisa watches with interest for what will happen next.

The small girl scowls and goes off toward her room. And Kate says, "Honestly, don't you sometimes wonder about being a mother? Why did we do it?" And she laughs.

Louisa senses that she is seeing something that in her experience is quite new. Whereas Grace Magowan always seems an "ideal mother" (and thus more than a little unreal), Kate comes across as simply honest: a mother who is uncertain about motherhood, and who (remarkably, for that pious period, the Eisenhower years) can say so.

But all this is only half-consciously perceived. Louisa is really thinking about Dan. Will he be at home? Will he want to see her?

Then—banging and pounding on the door, yelling "Mom!"—Stephen (whom Louisa has not seen before) arrives home. A big and sturdy five-year-old, who looks remarkably like Kate. He gazes coolly at Louisa, then says, "Hey, Mom, what's for lunch?"

(Stephen has one of those faces that change very little over the years: much later, at a party given by her daughter Maude, Louisa is to see Stephen—Stephen with Jennifer Magowan—and to know instantly who he is.)

Kate goes into the kitchen to feed her children, and Louisa tries Dan again. "Well, I'd counted on doing some work this afternoon," he tells her. He is writing a novel; he will not let her see anything that he has written, but it is important that she respect his effort.

"Well, okay."

"Christ," Dan says. "If you could just get out some-times at night! I'm so tired of this married-woman shit."

So is she, as she cannot say. She says instead, "I'll try, I'll think of something."

"Okay, kid. See you later."

Kate puts both her children down for naps, and then in the yellow kitchen she serves lunch to Louisa (a delicious shrimp curry).

"I always remember that marvelous chicken you made when I came to see you down on the Peninsula," Kate says, smiling.

Louisa can barely remember that evening; it is a discolored blur, among other blurs.

"Do you still see those people?" asks Kate. "Andrew something and his wife?"

Louisa makes an effort at recall. "Oh, the Chapins. Well, not really. Not since we moved up here."

"He called me once," Kate says. "It was strange."

And she tells Louisa.

Andrew called Kate, and reminded her of their meet-ing; he said that he had an appointment in town, and would she have lunch with him? ("Well, David had been away for so long, and I was so lonely that I would have had lunch with almost anyone.")

Andrew seemed excited, and much more animated than Kate remembered. He talked a lot about writing, about wanting to write, and preparing himself for that. All the novels in his mind. ("I had a terrible feeling that they would stay right there, inside his head.") A pleasant lunch, really, at a good French restaurant. Nothing untoward, nothing that could be construed as a pass (except the fact of the lunch itself, which *was* a pass, of course).

At the end Andrew thanked her for coming, and asked if they could meet again, and Kate said, well, perhaps not.

"I was really scared," Kate now tells Louisa. "I knew that I was very attracted to him, and I hadn't seen David for so long. If he'd really made a pass—I wonder. And later I thought about it; suppose we had gone to a motel and made love, would that have been so terrible? I mean if no one knew?"

Louisa murmurs something indistinct.

"He's very attractive. He reminded me a little of John."

"John?"

"John Jeffreys. Louisa, really." Kate muses, "But John was more definite, and God knows less serious, really. That fucking Southern charm. I don't think Andrew even knew what he wanted. And he kept talking about his children. Such a father!"

"Yes, he is."

"I don't see John as a father, somehow, do you? He'd manage to get out of it."

"I suppose."

For every reason this story, this conversation, has made Louisa very uncomfortable: it reminds her humiliatingly of Andrew ("Andrew, I love you," and then the taste of bile). Also how can she talk about making love? (It is a phrase that she does not use, not yet in her life: Michael has always talked about fucking, and that is what they do. Dan sometimes says, "Okay, kid, care to screw?") And how can she discuss the possibilities of unfaithfulness?

But for a wild moment she imagines telling Kate about Dan, how awful he is, how he doesn't love her at all. How terrible she feels, how worried about Maude. How she flinches from Michael's slightest touch.

She is too far gone, too sick (colitis was nothing to this depth of hopeless malaise) to realize that this would be a possible conversation; she is with a permanently affectionate friend. Who possibly could help.

Instead she begins to feel irritable with Kate, at what seems such a simple, pleasant, and unquestioning life.

And in a mean way she describes the visit to Michael. (The put-down of others is one of their few remaining sorts of conversation.)

"Well, Kate's become so ordinary. Another mother. I'm sure she hasn't opened a book for years. I don't know —she used to have a lot going, even a kind of originality. Or maybe I just thought so."

They smile at each other, momentarily united in their superiority to Kate and her boring life.

Dan leaves town, and Louisa finds a man who likes her even less than he did: a beautiful bisexual black man, a painter, named King.

"Can't you see that I despise you? To me you're an ugly white cunt, with no tits. Christ! I'm used to beauties."

Thus is Louisa addressed by King on a day near her

thirtieth birthday, a time that she feels to be the bottom of her life. (She is right.)

They are in King's apartment, a series of low dingy rooms, a basement. "Of course," he says. "I would have to live in a basement. Where else, outside of the Fillmore district?" King's color is golden bronze. In exchange for his room he does janatorial chores in the building, which he loathes.

"But she has a fever—I'm really sort of worried. I really should go." Desperate Louisa is speaking of Maude. She is standing at the sink, having just finished washing the dishes from King's dinner, having left the dishes from her own dinner in the sink, with Michael's and Maude's, rushed out of the house on some minor pretext.

"Go, go on ahead. Take care of your little baby daughter and your big baby husband."

She wipes her hands on a limp towel. "I guess fifteen or twenty minutes more won't make any difference. Do you want me to make coffee?"

"I had something a little more—uh—interesting than coffee in mind for this evening." He makes this very Southern, very Southern Negro, which he is not, with an evil, white-toothed grin.

But he is lying; she knows he is lying. He almost never wants to make love, and he never announces such a desire. It is she who persuades him with various blandishments. (They are all degrading, but this is not a word that she can allow into her mind. Not now.) She smiles, although her very facial muscles feel unconvinced.

"But I know I can't interest you in any such goings-on as that. Make the coffee—go ahead."

One of the myths of their "affair" (it is hardly that) is that of her nymphomania: she is supposed to be insatiable (for him) and at times she believes this to be true—God knows she is unsatisfied.

She makes the coffee while a small but very lively part of her mind, a part that she subdues, would like to throw it at him, scalding hot.

Why does she come to this terrible place, to wash dishes and to caress a passive crazy man who for the most part hates her? Louisa doesn't know; she doesn't think about it, any more than an addict thinks that his drug might be inferior. His passivity is her heroin.

He is stretched across the brown corduroy daybed, in his tight jeans, narcissistically bulging, and his white, white T-shirt. She brings the coffee to him there, placing it carefully on an upended orange crate, and she sits beside him —or rather near.

Suddenly he says, "You do have the nicest long hands and feet that I ever did see." A present: perhaps it is for such stray moments as this that she comes to him. She thrills to his praise, especially since he has said that the hands and feet of his great love, the vanished blond Bobbie, were chunky —fat. (Or maybe he likes fat feet? This occurs to her even as she is absorbing the compliment.) She also knows that he is using and will go on using any possible trick to make her stay. (When she has more time, he urges her to go.)

Louisa believes that he is an incredibly talented painter (she must believe). Canvases too high for the room are propped at intervals against the walls. A curious spectrum: shades of gray, and black and white are suddenly slashed with red. Violent and terrifying paintings, or beginnings of paintings: the most striking fact is that none of them is finished. On each canvas there is one small completed corner. But if he ever went on, the painting would be marvelous. (Louisa is sure of that.) Eventually King is to decide that the small corner is enough; he is perfect as he is.

Stretching toward her, King says, "How about it, baby. You feel like giving me a little blow before you go?"

She doesn't.

She does.

They met at a life class, at night, in a local art school. In the large cold room the skin of the naked model, who was fat, looked moist and white. Too ugly to draw, depressing. Louisa turned from the platform, looking for relief. And found King. He was seated a little below her, so that she was able to stare at him and to sketch his head without his knowledge. But of course he knew. She could also see his sketch of the fat model, whom he violently distorted: he made her fatter, more sagging, and somehow whiter, even colder than she looked in the flesh, and it came to Louisa that he must actually know and despise that woman.

Louisa didn't know King.

She thought that she had never seen a color as beautiful as the color of his skin. And warm—how marvelous to touch, to be allowed to touch!

(She assumed that he was a Negro, although she was not quite sure; he could have been something else, even Portuguese—she had never been to Portugal, and he was utterly unlike Negroes from Virginia.)

She wished that she had changed her clothes before coming to class. If he turned, he would see long dirty hair —she was too tired to wash it, and it took so long to dry—and a baggy sweater, over stained blue jeans. Clothes from college, ten years back. Now she looked like a beatnik.

After an hour and a half he turned and winked.

He let her drive him home. He invited her in, he

made coffee, and he told her all about a girl named Bobbie. How did Bobbie come up? Later Louisa could never remember.

"Just a fantastically beautiful young blond chick," he said. "That's all she was. Bobbie."

And Louisa's mind saw impossibly jutting, hard pale breasts, and a thatch of blond pubic hair. Did she, too, fall in love with Bobbie?

"With an inordinate zest for the sack. She had what you might call a veritable genius," he said, grinning sleepily, remembering God knows what pleasures, as Louisa wondered, Just what did she do that was so special? There are only so many holes, so many hands and tongues.

"But I had to go and fall in love with her. Up and down and out of my fucking mind in love, when she was thinking of fun and games."

Louisa's tired heart gave a lurch of sympathy; she could have done the same, fallen in love with someone who was having fun. Fun?

"Of course when I got so serious she pulled out." (She pulled out?) "Ran off to Europe with a couple of other guys." He chuckled tolerantly, with affection. "She was what you might call a switch hitter." Whatever that meant.

By this time Louisa was in love with King, and possibly with Bobbie as well. (Although later she is to decide that "Bobbie" is fictional—or is, quite possibly, "Bob.")

Breathlessly she asked, "Is she still there? In Europe?"

He gave her a studied, suspicious look. "As far as I know. Why?"

Cringingly, "I just wondered," she said.

They drank a lot of coffee and they tried to make love to each other, and none of the gestures of love worked out.

Both those things, the coffee and failed love, kept Louisa awake all night, at home, guiltily listening to Michael's heavy snores.

"Are you awake? I didn't wake you up?"

Michael has gone off to work, finally, and Maude taken to nursery school. Louisa telephones to King. She has told herself that he will feel badly about the night before, and that he should be reassured. (She is almost always wrong about King.)

"No, I was awake." He stretches and yawns; both are audible over the phone—his seductions. "I feel fine. What kind of a day is it?"

"Bright. Really pretty." She hesitates. "I thought if it was okay I'd come over and make breakfast for you. I could bring some things," she finishes vaguely.

"Well." He considers this proposition. Will he allow her to come and make his breakfast? He decides in her favor. "Well, okay. But I was planning on getting to work pretty soon."

"I'll be right there."

She races through the market (she has already washed her hair); she sweeps up delicacies into her cart. Smoked ham and mushrooms and imported jams; she forgets to buy eggs. She rushes across the city in the bright October weather (Thomas Wolfe weather); she parks and knocks on that basement door. Last night, in the dark, she had not noticed that it is painted red. Knocking there, waiting, she vaguely feels that the color is a warning.

King comes to the door, and in an awkward, embarrassed way they kiss.

He looks at the sack of groceries and gives her his evil

"Negro" grin. "I sure hope you've got some good old hominy in there. My mouth is really set for some good old grits. And eggs."

Christ! She has never had grits in her life. "Well, no," she says, lamely adding, "I didn't know you liked them."

"All us poor colored folks like grits—now didn't you know that?"

"But you're not Southern, are you?" She feels brave saying this.

"No, but you are." (What does this mean?)

Then he asks, "How much help did your folks have?"

"What?"

"You heard me: how many maids, and butlers and whatever. 'Help'—isn't that what you-all call them?"

"Uh—just one," she lies, and, as always with King, she has said the wrong thing. He would have preferred her surrounded by grinning echelons of black-faced servants.

"Oh, poor whites," he sneers.

"Well, not quite," she flickers; she is not quite dead.

She makes the breakfast, and he admits that it is pretty good. "But I never had any breakfast with no eggs."

She cleans up, and then there is an awkward moment during which she tries to look at her watch. She fails.

He says, "You got time for a quick screw?" He laughs, and then turns, instantly, dramatically (false) serious. "But I reckon by now you know that's not my style."

They meet mid-kitchen, they kiss. He says, "Shall we have an all-consuming love affair? Is that what you've got ahead of you, in your mind?"

She only smiles, feeling fleetingly pretty.

"Maybe you could take my mind right off that Bob—Bobbie—for me. Could you do that?"

Reaching, touching Louisa's tiny limp breasts, King thinks of Bobbie, of perfect generous flesh—or is this in Louisa's mind? Is it only she who thinks of Bobbie? Kissing her, he remembers a sweeter taste of Bobbie.

He talks a lot about Bobbie, encouraged by Louisa. "She dressed like a kind of premature beatnik," he says. (King hates beatniks: a bunch of dirty white kids, a lot of them Jews—what do they know about street life?) "She wore sweat shirts and jeans, old sneakers. I wanted her to dress up pretty, of course. In cashmere sweaters and pearls, and I bought her that stuff."

(Did he? Is this true?)

"But wouldn't she wear it, to please you?"

"Are you kidding—Bobbie? Not that kid." As always, his voice is full of admiration. (But is it *true*, or is Bobbie his creation?)

And then there are moments when it seems to both of them that they are involved in a violent love affair (although somewhat fictional). Recklessly she comes to him in the middle of the night, having with no valid excuse abandoned Michael at a party of psychologists in Park Merced. She claims to be exhausted, she is going home, and she forcefully insists that Michael stay on; as usual her hysteria convinces him—she is still powerful over him.

In her tight black dress that Caroline had sent for Christmas, perfumed and smelling of booze, she comes to King, all out of breath. "I couldn't stand it without seeing you, not another minute."

"Christ, you're great," he says. "I couldn't have stood the night if you didn't come."

Then they make love frenziedly, not removing many clothes; they spend longer over their farewells, their lingering (fictional) lovers' good nights, than they did in the act of love.

"You were lovely to come. Dream of me."

"Yes, I love you."

This is how lovers behave, they believe—passionate lovers. But is that what they are doing, acting out love?

And then he tells her that he despises her.

He criticizes the way she has an orgasm. "Most women I've known"—and of course he means Bobbie—"most women, it's like they've been struck by lightning. But you—I can hardly tell."

How can she say to him that she hardly ever comes with him? She pretends to, and she doesn't want or dare to overact. She has to be as sexy, as womanly, as Bobbie. And more so.

"Fucking you is like fucking someone black," he says, his voice full of anger and despair.

This makes sense to Louisa. I have a black woman's cunt, is what she thinks.

Sometimes she sneaks home to Michael, aroused and unfulfilled, and she manages to arouse him. To come. The smallest twitch.

She is loathsome to herself.

The thought of her daughter is unbearable to her. Maude cries a lot. She doesn't like other children. In the sandbox at the playground she used to throw sand and fight over toys; she was unable to "share." Nowadays she is listless, watching television all afternoon. No friends.

And the worst of it is that Maude will have to grow up, grow into being a woman, needing men. She will fall in love with men, over and over. Falling.

Louisa thinks that it would have been much better if she had had a son. God, she could have loved a son!

Some innate fastidiousness prevents Louisa from talking in detail to King about Michael ("that fat Jew you married"), but King somehow intuits Michael through her. "I'll bet he spends a lot of time in the can, doesn't he?" This is a thing she would never have mentioned.

She blushes.

"Ah, you're blushing. You know, you're really pretty when you blush."

She thinks about Michael as little as possible, even when they are together. Then she is thinking about King.

She does not think about the rest of her life.

Once, only once, she breaks down with King; she cries out to him, "I can't stand my life! I live in a nightmare, I despise Michael. It's killing me. I'm killing Maude."

He eyes her evilly. "Don't you look at me, baby," he says. "I can't help you, not at all. I've got my own brown skin to save."

She wonders if he is right, that she was asking him to save her. Very likely, but she isn't sure.

"How about giving me a little blow before you go?"

She does.

. . .

A check from her mother, from Caroline. For her birthday. The bottom of her life. She wonders if she could possibly tell Caroline how she feels; would Caroline send her money if she got a divorce and a part-time job? But she doesn't know how to type.

She goes to Magnin's; she buys a pale blue cashmere sweater, a matching tweed skirt, and a rope of pearls. Driving to King's basement, she has a curious sense of impersonation; she is dressed up to be someone else. And then of course it comes to her: at an intersection where she watches a pretty young blond girl cross the street. (Is that Bobbie? She is always looking for Bobbie, as she imagines that King is always looking.) At that moment she understands she is wearing the clothes that King said he bought for Bobbie (that, even to please him, Bobbie refused to wear). The sick complexity of this weighs her down, so that by the time she gets to King she is not a pretty young woman in pretty, expensive new clothes; she is a terrified anxiety-filled young-old person, perhaps a woman.

Of course he notices. "That's a new style of dress for you, now, isn't it? But I'm not sure you're really the type for it. I like those classic clothes on a body that's a little more —voluptuous—"

Whatever King says has a special ironic undertone; he is almost never direct. Considering this, Louisa is dimly reminded of someone else, someone who also speaks in a stilted way, as though always kidding, which he is not. Who says mean things as though they were a joke.

And then it comes to her: Jack Calloway, her father. Jesus *Christ*.

. . .

They only see each other in King's basement. They have given up the art class, King because he decided it was no good ("What do those mothers know?"), and Louisa because she can use the time to see King, pretending to continue with the class.

The city outside, lovely San Francisco, might not exist at all; they could be in St. Louis, or Iowa Falls. Along Grant Avenue the beatniks are slowly vanishing; it is never clear where they have gone, and their hangouts slowly die: Miss Smith's Tea Room, the Bagel Shop, The Place. King and Louisa have never been in a bar together, or walked along a street. The city's skyline is still gentle, more Mediterranean than Manhattan in its aspect—no greedy Mafia-shadowed mayor yet, no greedy builders. Alex Magowan and the other engineers are just starting out. It is the end of the fifties, in a reasonably quiet city.

Curiously, King always praises the small sketches that Louisa does; he encourages her to draw. "You've got one delicate Southern touch," he tells her. "And class. Style. You're a real Southern lady artist."

This is praise; she knows that her Southernness is what (if anything) he likes in her, although he often taunts her: "I don't reckon your folks would be too happy for me to come by for a little visit, now, would they?"

For some reason, which at first Louisa does not understand, King asks her repeatedly about Kate. Their friendship. She has told him about the naked swimming —the night of sex appeal, and how they laughed. He keeps going back to that night.

"You just laughed and fell in the water and then got out and dressed?"

"Well, yes."

He makes a sound of disbelief as he looks at her curiously.

Embarrassed, and not sure why (but sure that she is failing him again), Louisa limply says, "Really. That's all."

Softly: "Really?"

She understands that he is (of course) suggesting a lesbian scene—and it is not an accusation. It is something he wants very much; he would like to watch her with Kate. And she has a queasy memory of something that Michael once said: "Homosexual . . . you and Kate."

It even, for a moment, occurs to her to improvise, to make up such a scene, as a present for him.

But then, "Really, that was all," she says, in total defeat. "Nothing happened."

One November morning, in her pretty cashmere clothes, Louisa goes downtown; she has nothing else to wear, and she has to buy a birthday present for Michael. Dispiritedly she enters Brooks Brothers.

Gazing unhappily at the neat stacks of regimental striped ties at her elbow, she suddenly hears, "Louisa—Lou, it's really you—terrific!"

And there is Andrew Chapin, dark handsome Andrew, old friend and former neighbor. Andrew with his heavy crooked eyebrows and his grin. (It is several minutes before she remembers that humiliating party scene; at first she is simply glad to see him.)

They don't embrace, possibly because they are in Brooks Brothers, and alone. They make enthusiastic embracing gestures at each other. How marvelous to see you, they both say.

Andrew says, "Louisa, you're so pretty. Really, you look great." And then he says, "Say, I don't suppose you're free for lunch."

Lunch. She's free for anything, really.

He takes her to an elegant, New York–style restaurant (the one to which he also took Kate), a place that in years to come will be leveled to make way for a towering Hyatt House.

Across from each other at the small table, in the dim subdued room where ladies are wearing beautiful large hats, Louisa and Andrew smile foolishly at each other in embarrassed pleasure and surprise.

"Well," they say simultaneously, "how is—" and they both laugh.

"You first," Andrew tells her. "Michael—and Maude?"

This is depressing. "Michael's fine," she says quickly. "You know he got his degree finally? But his parents—" She instantly decides not to say anthing about Michael's parents, those appalling monstrous monoliths, and in that instant she realizes how difficult it is to say anything about Michael without mentioning his parents. King, an orphan, was raised by an aunt, whom he never talks about. And Andrew never talks about his famous father.

"And Maude? I'd really like to see her."

"She's fine. She's funny—she writes poems all the time. Sometimes limericks. You want to hear one? You wouldn't mind?"

"No, really."

And Louisa recites:

"There once was a pig named Sam
  Who shook when someone mentioned ham
  When someone mentioned bacon
  He went right on shakin'
  And when pork was mentioned he ran."

"She wrote that? But that's terrific."

"Well, I know it's awful to quote your kids." She laughs. "Michael thinks it's anti-Semitic." Of course this is untrue; she is trying to be funny, and it works. Andrew laughs hard, his quirky eyebrows raised. "How are Sally and the boys?"

Everyone is fine; no one seems to have changed at all. Why do they no longer see each other? This question lies between them, insufficiently answered by the fact that Michael and Louisa have moved up to San Francisco.

They have drinks, but it is being with Andrew that makes Louisa high; she is elated, she feels herself transformed. And later, remembering that lunch, it becomes an almost holy event. "Andrew sort of saved my life, that day," she tells John Jeffreys, whom many years later she loves, and marries. "I'd lost track of who I was."

Wanting to know everything (really everything about Andrew), Louisa even asks about the Magowans.

"They've had a lot of trouble with Allison—that's the middle kid," says Andrew, and Louisa remembers a shy and too thin little girl, with scabs always on her bony knees (who couldn't think where to hide Easter eggs, until her wonderful mother, Grace, told her where).

"She's really sick," says Andrew. "Sally says she won't eat and she throws up all the time."

"Anorexia," Louisa mechanically says. Michael has explained that it is the opposite of ("and of course that makes it related to") her colitis.

"What's weird is that Grace makes it sound like a bad cold, and Alex never mentions it at all. It makes it hard to be with them."

"I'll bet. 'Denial' is what Michael would say they're doing."

But Louisa is too happy to talk about the Magowans, or Michael; she has already forgotten what Andrew has just told her about them.

What would Andrew say, she wonders at some point, if she told him that she was in love with a Negro, committing adultery with a Negro man? (Screwing and getting screwed by one.) But she is not, not now, in love with King. She despises him; she wishes he were dead.

She asks, "And, Andrew, what about you? Are you writing a lot?"

A sad smile. "Not really. I seem to spend all my time winding up to write, and then not. And you know, Sally and the boys—not that it's their fault that I don't write," he says ambiguously.

And then he says, "Louisa, Lou—I don't know how to say this, but I'd give five years of my life to go back to that time—that time with you. Jesus, what a stuffy ass I was."

He takes her hand, very gently.

Louisa feels her face heating, her blood race. It is impossible to look at Andrew.

"If only—don't you think we could?" he says softly (and too vaguely). He has no clear plan. He is not saying: "Let's walk out to the lobby and take a room in the hotel upstairs."

And so she has to say no (and besides her slip is torn and pinned together). She says, "Andrew, I'm afraid I have to get home—Maude—" (And she is fastidious, in her way: she is seeing King that night.)

"Of course. But may I call you sometime?"

"Sure." (But he does not.)

Beyond her slip and Andrew's uncertainty, the truth is that at this time Louisa does not feel that she "deserves" Andrew—she does not deserve an extremely bright and attractive man. (Just as, years back, she would not have felt that she deserved John Jeffreys. He was for attractive Kate, and she was grateful for Richard.)

"Well," Andrew now says, "care for dessert, or coffee?"

"I guess not. No—no thanks."

It has become embarrassingly important to get away from each other; suddenly there is nothing more to say. The waiter takes an inordinate amount of time with the check, it seems (and they both privately wonder if he is misinterpreting their haste).

Their cars are in separate garages, Louisa's under Union Square, Andrew's in a smaller (more expensive) garage off Kearny Street. And so at the entrance to Louisa's garage they exchange hurried goodbyes.

Louisa gets her car with unusual speed, and even in the moment of driving out onto Geary Street she is beset with a total change of mind (or instinct or heart). Why *shouldn't* she and Andrew make love? Why not, this afternoon? She loves Andrew (in a way); she always has. What would he care about a pin in her slip? Everyone does that sometimes; certainly Sally does. She could turn right, turn right again on Post Street, and go down to Kearny. Easy to find Andrew there waiting for his car—in a gay way to say, "Guess what, I've changed my mind. Where shall we go?"

But the lights are with her; she hurries along Geary Street, never turning right, until she reaches Van Ness Avenue, by which time it would be too late—probably.

Instead she spends a miserable afternoon (cross with Maude) of self-recrimination and regret.

As Andrew does. Speeding down the Bayshore (Michael's idea of hell, and at this moment Andrew would agree), he wonders why (WHY?) he didn't say:"Look, you have coffee and I'll go and register at the hotel. I'll say you're joining me in ten or fifteen minutes. Lou—okay?"

If he had said that, she would have shyly smiled and said yes—he knows her; he is sure of that. Louisa would at least sometimes like to be told what to do. (Andrew thinks that is a mistake that Michael makes with her.)

Or—he could have taken her in his car out Lombard Street, to one of the motels there.

By the time he gets home, he has worked out the mechanics of that possible afternoon in innumerable ways. It is depressingly clear that it was all his fault that nothing happened.

"Well, you're looking pretty sassy tonight," King says later—horrifyingly: this is a favorite phrase of Louisa's father.

And then he says, "What happened? You run into some kind of an old friend downtown?"

How could he have known? "Oh, you saw us?"

"I haven't been out of the house." This is probably true; King almost never goes out except at night, and then, almost invisible, he roams. (He mentions gyms on Market Street; he does not mention hustling outside downtown hotels.) "I just guessed," he says.

He is a witch, a warlock; she has always known this about him. She admits, "Yes, in fact I had lunch with an old friend."

"Well, now, that's all right; you don't have to apologize."

"I'm not."

He has sprawled as usual across his couch, in his invariable clean white T-shirt. His eyes are large and luminous and tired. His mouth is tight.

Louisa sits, as always, uncomfortably forward on a stiff chair; she has thrown her coat across the couch, near King's feet. Tonight the room looks strange to her, as King looks strange. (Why is she here?)

He says, "Well, I can't exactly object to that. Matter of fact an old friend of mine blew into town, blew over to see me, if you don't mind the expression." He yawns, by way of emphasis, and then he watches Louisa.

She has a curious sense that he is lying; Bobbie was not there that afternoon, if indeed there is a Bobbie. In any case the old thrilling and addictive anxiety, usually stirred by any shadow of Bobbie, is missing now. Louisa simply looks at King (who is he?), and then she does what it is amazing that she has never done before: she picks up her coat and without a word she goes out the door.

This is not the end of it, not quite. King telephones, of course, and they act out a violent reconciliation.

This happens again.

And again.

By then it is late spring, a lovely May in which Louisa takes Maude on picnics, and long country drives to see the flowering trees. They spend afternoons at windy beaches that remind her of home, of beaches in Maryland and Virginia. It is an exceptional spring.

Louisa is working hard. Dozens of drawings, and she is thinking about drawing all the time.

(And she is on the verge of understanding that King and the others have been excuses for not leaving Michael.)

King decides to take his paintings (still unfinished) to

New York, in fact to move there. He insists that Louisa follow him—he is madly in love with her by now. And she agrees, wondering if this is what she will do.

He telephones, he writes. Once he simply arrives. He has flown back to see her, if only for an afternoon.

She tells him that it is over; she is through. Such simple (and final) knowledge; she is just not glad to see him.

But King is insanely perverse. He continues to telephone, even when she hangs up at the sound of his voice. And some uncanny instinct, some lingering sense of her, makes him always telephone in moments of crisis—Louisa's crisis. He calls when she is waiting for a call from Bayard, who comes close to breaking her heart.

He calls just after she has learned that her mother has died.

He is a ghost, who for years will haunt her life.

Seven / 1960

Late night, Louisa's bedroom. It is also Michael's bedroom, but for the past two years he has been sleeping in his study. Working there, he would fall asleep over books or periodicals. Then, for a time, his practice was to get up and come to the bed where Louisa already was. If she was at home. She was often out: art classes, movies with friends. Things like that. Out, home late.

Louisa has persuaded Michael that she hates to be awakened in the middle of the night. Can't go back to sleep.

But tonight—having freshly showered and shaved, brushed teeth—he goes into the still dark room. Wanting her.

They have not made love for—he can't remember when. (Ten months—she could remember; she could have told him that.)

He sits on the bed, knowing she is not asleep, waiting for her to stop pretending that she is.

He touches her hand, at which she retracts it; she

pulls her knees up to her chest and clutches them, as she opens her eyes.

He touches her foot. "I want to make love to you, to kiss—."

She pulls back the foot. "I think we should get a divorce."

A harsh and unreal sentence, curiously loud. A sentence that continues to hang in the dark between them, with its own existence—or so Michael feels it.

Weakly he says, "What?"

"A divorce," she repeats, as though making a reasonable demand. Expressing a choice.

Michael is suddenly aware that outside their windows (theirs?—hers?) a torrential rain has begun, lashing at the glass, creaking through the bones of the house. Playing for time—he is waiting for something, anything else to happen—he remarks on this. "It's raining."

"Yes."

No help. Knowing how stupid he must sound, he says, "I can't believe this is happening to us."

She doesn't answer, although he can feel her looking at him, and so he says something worse: "I thought in some ways we had a good marriage."

She makes a short bitter sound. Then she says, "Christ, Michael."

It occurs to him to say, Well, why not make love anyway? For once. What could it matter?

But even as these brave and uncharacteristic sentences form he realizes that he no longer wants to. Couldn't, in fact, even if she did.

So that now there is simply the question of what else to say. And since there is nothing else, how to get out of the room. He begins to inch backward on the bed; then, aware that he is moving much too slowly, ridiculously, he suddenly stands up. He dimly feels that the less that is said the better. The quickest, perhaps, forgotten.

He says, "Well, see you in the morning."

"Goodnight."

It is barely possible that she is crying. He can't tell.

The next day is a clear soft warm April day. It is bright enough to make the previous night unreal, and all that day Michael tries to tell himself (amazing, how nearly he succeeds in believing) that the night before did not, in fact, occur. Louisa did not say what, in the midst of the midnight storm, he thought he heard her say.

Ironically, most of the patients whom he sees that day are people with marital problems. (Or perhaps this is what everyone has? They "come and go"—are not serious?)

"Doctor, we don't communicate—."

"Doctor, it's been four years since we—."

"Doctor, just what is the difference between a psychologist and a psychiatrist?"

(Michael hates this question; for one thing, he is so tired of it.)

"Wasserman, what the hell kind of a name is that, *if* you don't mind my asking."

"Doctor, my father never did—."

"—and now it's too late."

When he gets home, Louisa and Maude have just got back from the park, and their faces are a little pink from the unusual sun. Especially Maude's since she is fairer. They are both cheerful and slightly out of breath, having had a good afternoon.

Remembering the night before, and for a moment

quite sure that it was real—she *did* say that—Michael looks at Maude and feels a stabbing pain at the possibility of her loss. He goes over to her and strokes her fair hair. His own color hair. His child. "Honey, would you like me to read to you for a while?"

Louisa gives him an opaque look, but she says, "Terrific. I'll get dinner."

Chicken and rice. Asparagus. A green salad. Coconut cake (a bought one—Sara Lee). A dinner like any other.

Conversation, or lack of it, like any other. The two adults speak mainly to Maude. Michael for the first time notices this, and makes an attempt to talk to Louisa, to his wife. "I had a real old-fashioned anti-Semite of a patient today," he begins, chuckling—she will like this story.

Maude interrupts. "Why are patients called 'patients'?"

Interested, their attention caught, her parents stare at each other. Why, indeed, why patients? Odd that they had never thought of it.

Encouraged, Maude asks, "What do patients have to do with patience?"

Michael explains. "Both words are from the Latin root, the word for suffering, or enduring—." But in the course of his explanation to Maude he has forgotten the story he meant to tell Louisa. Something about an anti-Semite, a patient? At that, a heavy vision of his mother intrudes on his mind, and he thinks of all that Louisa has suffered (and endured) at the hands of his parents. He sighs, unaware that he is imitating his mother's heavy sighs.

That is how things are for a week or so: no more communication but, on the other hand, no less. And what Michael least wants to do is to push the issue.

Then one afternoon he comes home to find Louisa also just home, and all dressed up and very excited. "Really, terrific news," she tells him. She is very pretty in her navy suit, sweater, and pearls—in her excitement. 'I've got a job!"

"Honey, that's great." But his heart lurches sideways: what does this mean, a job?

She describes a small advertising agency in an old building in North Beach. "Of course at first I'll just be doing layouts, comprehensives and the salary isn't much—."

She goes on for some time, animatedly, after Michael has stopped listening: he is too anxious to listen to what she says. What will it mean, her having a job?

Clearly she has thought of everything: arranged for Maude to stay with a friendly neighbor for a couple of hours after school, and since it is only a part-time job Louisa will be home at two. And next fall Maude will be in school till two. She is going to see about a cleaning lady.

Louisa starts work the next Monday. When Michael comes home, she is there, with Maude, her stockinged feet in bedroom slippers. "God, I'm really tired!" But from the kitchen comes the satisfying warm garlicky smell of a carefully prepared casserole.

She talks a lot at dinner. She is nervy, excited. Tired, but her eyes are lighter than they have been for years. (What does this mean?) Michael can hardly listen to anything that she is saying.

Spring.

Summer.

. . .

Nothing happens. Except that one day Michael notices that Louisa never goes anywhere at night any more, no more movies with friends. But he can't remember how long she has not been doing this.

She gets a lot of special delivery letters from New York, but what could that possibly mean?

During the days of his most acute anxiety, some cruel quirk in Michael's mind makes him think only of the best times with Louisa; the bad days are unavailable to his needful memory. The first time they screwed, in the attic of his parents' house in Boston, with his parents right downstairs! Louisa in a black dress, very animated, at a party. Introducing Louisa to Dr. Sampson. Sampson's face.

But slowly over the summer, Michael's anxiety diminishes. The cold San Francisco summer seems to last, and nothing changes. Perhaps nothing is going to change. Louisa goes to work; she cheerfully complains that she is tired. She goes to bed early. They all go to bed early. Separately.

Then, early in September, Louisa tells Michael excitedly that on a sudden impulse she has called her old friend Kate. ("You remember Kate? She came down to see us for dinner, when I was pregnant." He does, but not quite: someone sexy, something unpleasant.) Kate now lives in Berkeley; her husband is a surgeon—hearts. They have a house near Tahoe, and have invited Louisa for a week. Louisa and Maude. "I told them you couldn't get away." And so they go. (The agency is nice about letting Louisa take time off, with no pay.)

Michael does not like being alone; he finds it frightening, a silence full of echoes. He eats a lot—snacks, several meals a day. But he decides that he is really all right; it is temporary. His wife and daughter are away on a visit.

He thinks that the thing to do is to make a celebration of their return. Louisa has sometimes remarked that he is "joyless"—his is not a festive sensibility. He is not Southern, with all their ceremonies and effusions.

He goes out to buy champagne, although at the last minute he cannot remember which one Louisa has said is best, Korbel or Almadén. (French champagne would be going too far, really; it would show desperation.) He decides on Almadén, but is sure that he has made the wrong decision. He remembers to put glasses in the refrigerator. He considers calling a baby-sitter, so that he can take Louisa out to dinner, but then is struck with a better idea; he will take them both out. Safer that way. A reunited family.

And they go to a family-style restaurant, brown Louisa and Maude and pale Michael, who feels fat; can he have gained weight in a week? (he has.) A French-Italian restaurant, where you get a lot to eat. On the walls are amateurish reproductions of famous paintings, but the effect is warm.

At first Maude and Louisa talk a lot. How cold the lake was. Water skiing—Louisa surprised herself by being good at it. "*Sort* of. But I must be feeling really confident these days." She smiles. Sailing. Kate's children. Busy David, the successful doctor. "Really repairing *hearts.*" Kate's intense domesticity. "But she seems really happy doing all that, and the kids are nice. The youngest is named for me—I was touched."

Then it all seems to fizzle down, their talk, and they might not have been away, Louisa and Maude. The three of them could be any tired family, out hopefully for dinner.

They go home.

Maude goes to bed.

With a sort of bravado Michael brings in the champagne. Chilled glasses on a tray. "I thought we ought to celebrate your coming home," he says. "But I can't remember if it was Korbel or Almadén we liked."

"Korbel."

"Oh." His weak smile. "Oh, well."

She clears her throat. "Michael, we have to see about getting a divorce."

"But—" But there is nothing for him to say. He looks at her stupidly, quite aware that that is what he is doing. Then he says what is at least half true. "I thought you'd changed your mind."

"Michael! How could we go on living together? How could we? There isn't anything—nothing—."

Almost unconsciously, because he has opened it and it is there, they are sipping their wine.

He says, "Couldn't we just—go on?"

"Go on where? With no sex? I've been—unfaithful to you. Often. And I hate being like that."

His face has become very hot. "I don't believe you." (But, like most pieces of sexual information, this one has always been somewhere within him, a submerged knowledge.) "What do you mean, unfaithful?"

"Just that. Screwing other people. All kinds." Her voice runs out of power, trails off. She has made a great effort to say what she is saying. Or perhaps she is lying?

"I don't believe you," Michael says again.

With her hands she makes a small despairing gesture. "Okay, don't. But what's terrible is how little you notice. Anything."

He hesitates, knowing that whatever he says will somehow be used against him. He says, "I don't know what you mean."

"Exactly." She sighs, with an infinite and terrible weariness. It is clear that she is most of all tired of Michael.

And clear from her eyes that she pities him. But in his pain he will accept even pity. Very simply he says, "I don't know what to do."

"Michael, if you could only see how much better off you'll be without me. I'm terrible for you, and I can't stop. You could marry someone who loves you." For an instant she brightens. "You could marry Persephone Taylor. I think she has a sort of crush on you. And she's so rich."

"I could never marry anyone who looks like that." (He does.) But for the moment he is barely thinking about Persephone. He is thinking: I could never be married to anyone but you.

Miserably (for the moment) he believes this to be true.

Eight / 1961

(Maude's later memory of herself and her parents at that time.)

When she first came home in the afternoon, just after she got a part-time job in an advertising agency and she and my father were divorced, she would make herself a long drink of bourbon with a lot of ice. Louisa, my mother. She would put the drink on the coffee table and then bring in the phone, with its long coiled and twisted cord, and put the box on the floor beside her and pick up the receiver, and dial and listen and talk. Or sometimes she would pick up the phone and walk around with it; she did that most often when she was talking to someone whom she didn't like, or who bored her (my father, Michael; or, later, my father and Persephone, his wife). Then she would make terrible private faces that only I could see, and she would gesture with the phone, raising and lowering it like a barbell.

From so much moving, the long cord became impossibly twisted. Just lying on the floor it would twitch—a snake. I sometimes thought that if I had been a boy and very angry at my mother I would have cut that cord with some heavy clippers, and she would say, "What a little devil he is!"—although that does not sound like Louisa. It was not that I especially wanted to be a boy, but I imagined that boys and their mothers got along in a simpler way than Louisa and I did.

When my program was over, or a few minutes after, I would go into the living room and stand there, and when she saw me she would smile in a wide bright way and say into the phone, "Excuse me—here's Maude," and then, to me, "Darling, how are you? What kind of a day did you have?"

I would tell her a few things, really wanting her to go on talking to her friend. As she did, too, but neither of us could do what we wanted to. That was how we were with each other, at that time.

This was when I was nine or so and my mother was in her early thirties. On TV I watched teen-age dance times in the afternoons: very wholesome kids rocking gently, far apart from each other, pausing to refresh themselves with soft drinks. They were only a few years older than me, but I couldn't believe that I would soon be like them, the way (I then thought) I was supposed to. It was frightening: how else would I be?

Sometimes in the mornings I would play sick or cut school to watch daytime serials with names like "Brighter Day" or "Shining Hour" or "Storm Clouds." I knew that I never would be like those people, either, but that was less frightening; I somehow also knew I wasn't supposed to. I could lose myself in almost any world—except, of course, my own and my mother's.

My mother, Louisa, was (still is) tall and thin, and in her own way beautiful, with dark hair and nice skin, and large eyes. Green-shadowed eyes. In those days she was excited about being "free" (free except for me). She suddenly knew a lot of men who took her out to dinner, and it would all have been fine except that she worried so much: about money (my father had got the better deal out of the divorce, and Persephone was rich); about me (she needn't have—I was really okay); about getting baby-sitters when she went out; and about the fact that she didn't really care much about any of the men she knew. My mother is always worried about something.

"Well, he's nice enough," she would say into the phone. "We have a good time but I come home and think, So what? Why bother? I could just as easily stay home with Maude. I can't believe that I left Michael for this 'dating' scene. I do wonder what I want."

I knew what she wanted, and maybe she did, too: she wanted a full-scale melodrama, like the ones that I watched on the twelve-inch screen.

My father, who didn't want the divorce, was almost immediately taken up by rich fat Persephone. He moved to a flat on Lombard Street, where it curls down Russian Hill, and Persephone lived near there. She kept inviting him in for expensive food; she seemed to spend most of her time doing a sort of food research, and then buying and cooking it all, and she loved to talk about food. "There was a special small cake we used to have at home, in Madison," she would say, "but I can't quite remember the seasoning. It *could* have been coriander."

I was a disappointment, a discouragement to Persephone, because in those days I did not like to eat very much. I was bored with all food, even the special little cakes with which she tried to woo me, along with my father. It was terribly important to Persephone that I like her, which was dumb: although he *loves* me overwhelmingly, my father isn't interested in my opinions; my mother's were more than he could cope with. He is not a good listener.

As though to atone for my not eating, he ate enough for both of us. I also had an impression that he was trying to be as fat as Persephone was, and finally, by the time they were married, that is more or less what happened: he was enormous, from croissants, brioche, caviar, and Béarnaise and heavy wine. In fact they came to sort of look alike.

While my parents were still married, I had an idea that Michael, my father, would have liked to be Louisa, my mother. At parties at our house when she told stories, laughing and gesturing a lot, I would watch his face, and he seemed to be wishing that he were like her. And once—this was really peculiar—a man from a newspaper who was writing an article on "young suburban mothers" (we were then living on the Peninsula) came to interview my mother, and my father answered all the questions: "Well, Louisa usually shops around mid-afternoon. She draws. Her drawings are mostly of people." My mother did not interrupt (being polite is important to Louisa), but she looked at him as though she did not want to believe what he was doing.

They didn't fight, but the air between them was heavy and gray-dead. My mother came to life when there were other people around; then she joked and talked a lot, frantically gay. But she had a lot of trouble sleeping (a long time ago she had been really sick), and most mornings she couldn't get up for a while (which perhaps is one reason that Persephone always made a point of inviting my father for breakfast: lox and bagels, potato pancakes, German crêpes).

I didn't mind living in the suburbs as much as my mother did. I had some friends, and in the summer we squirted each other with hoses in the back yards, and our mothers took us to playgrounds, and for walks across the golf course. We went for picnics in the state parks or to the beach, where usually it was too cold. I preferred the park picnics, at long tables in huge dark groves of redwoods, near a stream with ferny banks.

We did not have TV then, and since I was too young to have seen many other people I did not recognize my parents' marriage as being "bad." It is only later when I remember their faces, how they looked at each other, that I see her unhappiness and his passive but total confusion.

And so they were divorced and they moved to different parts of San Francisco: my rich father to curly Lombard Street, my mother to our fringe Pacific Heights flat. Her courage only went so far.

What would she have done without the telephone? I have wondered about that. I remember a terrible afternoon in the last days of Bayard (Bayard the Bad, as I came to think of him) when the phone was out of order and no one could fix it until the *next day*. She stared at it, physically hovering around that small black corded box, as though it were a sick person who might return to life with enough care. It would have been absolutely impossible for her to leave it alone and go for a walk, the sensible thing which even a character in "Brighter Day" would have done.

The first I ever hear of Bayard was from my mother, speaking to her friend Kate over the phone. She said, "Really, these married men who meet you at parties and then call up. What do they think? Someone named Bayard has called me three times this week."

Before she met Bayard, and for the brief period after that during which she was still her own woman, my mother and I were quite successfully passing in our roles: she was the stylish divorcée who went out a lot, and I was a young girl who watched too much TV, and at school with the other girls I pretended to be afraid of boys. But I was not afraid of boys, really, and sometimes I felt a kind of separation from the other girls. I have no idea what my mother felt about herself.

"And this is my daughter, Maude," my mother said, clinging to me in what seemed an unnatural way. She was speaking to the largest man I had ever seen, a florid giant with thick red hair. Bayard. I disliked him on sight, which my sentimental mother attributed to some knowledge that he would hurt her. Not so: I simply don't like arrogant, oversized people.

He did not like me, either. "Well, how do you do, young lady," he said, with his eyes cold and pale blue. He had pale pink freckles all over his hands. Kate and Stephen, although they have red hair, do not have freckles.

"You can stay in the living room with us, Maude, if you like," my mother pleaded with me.

But I turned her down cold. "I've got a lot of homework to do," I lied.

"I'll only stay a minute," promised Bayard—falsely, as things turned out. She should have known, or perhaps she did.

At dinner that night, an hour and a half later, my mother was flushed and angrily excited. Very attractive. "I simply couldn't get rid of him!" she kept saying. "The nerve. Just because he's used to pushing people around."

At that time, and for months afterward, my mother and I pretended that I did not know who Bayard was, which was fairly dumb. I read the papers, and there he always was: civic leader, opera patron, owner of, married to, seen at—all that. My poor mother had met her match.

As though our flat were a small country containing

something that he could use, Bayard invaded it, and us. There was a saturation bombardment of phone calls, telegrams, and flowers. He favored flowers with aggressive shapes: birds-of-paradise, and gladioli. These were in fact my mother's least favorite flowers, but her enthusiasm was convincing, even to me. He often showed up at the door—a surprise attack. An incursion.

For a while she struggled, using rather pathetic ruses such as having me answer the phone and say she was out, or inviting a friend to come for tea when he was supposed to arrive. But it was an unequal fight.

I came home from school one afternoon, on a day that my mother had stayed in bed with a slight flu, and from the disarray in her room or some vibration that she gave off I knew that Bayard had just left, and that the scene between them had been decisive—the decision his.

During dinner, for which she got up, she showed a funny tendency to giggle, and God knows I was not being especially funny. I was curiously watching her. The phone rang several times that evening, and each time she answered, and it was Bayard, and they had breathless brief conversations during which she said silly things: "Yes I, too. Incredible. Yes. Tomorrow. A miracle."

(Much later, when she was being funny again, my mother said to Kate, "I only hope that God protects me from any more miracles.")

After that I began to watch my mother in earnest. I even lost interest in most television programs. Her drama was far more real, and it went on all day long.

He came at odd hours, Bayard did, and I think without calling first. Often he appeared late in the afternoon, and so my mother no longer came home from work to make a drink and sit down to telephone her friends. Instead she rushed to the bathroom to wash up, and then she sat at her dressing table doing unnecessary things to her face and hoping that he would come. Needless to say, when he did I was no longer urged to stay in the living room; I was firmly reminded of homework and (contradictorily) of favorite TV programs.

Under such treatment I "regressed," or so my guilty mother saw it. The truth is that I was interested in what was going on. And so I would slide into the living room and whine, "When's dinner, Mom?" and see them tear apart from their embrace.

Poor mother, poor Louisa—certainly she still blames herself for this period of my life, and feels that it marked and marred me. And there has never been a way to tell her that she is wrong, that on the contrary she provided me with more entertainment than most children my age got, those who had to live through the fifties with only TV to watch.

Since all his notices in the papers indicated that Bayard was extremely rich, I had fantasies of my mother in mink (which she would have thought extremely tacky—a word she liked) or at least of my mother being able to quit her advertising job—a job she didn't like, that did not pay well, and that left no time for her own drawings, which had been important to her. But nothing of the sort ever happened. In fact the flowers stopped coming early on, and the only contribution that I noticed were occasional bottles of Scotch, which is what Bayard drank. My mother, being Southern, favored bourbon.

Watching them, as I continuously did, I tried fervently to figure out why. Why had they chosen each other? Why my mother for Bayard, and him for her? At that time most people struck me as interchangeable.

But there they were, ravenously upon each other on

the sofa in the late afternoons, and sometimes I would wake at night to hear his steps creaking down the hall toward my mother's room.

Whether by agreement or not (there was no way for me to find this out), my mother stopped going out to dinner with other men. Perhaps he insisted; perhaps she was afraid of missing one of his visits. Either (or both) is possible. But she had thrown out any pretense of equal rights. She was fully engaged in acting out her love affair.

What opposite directions my parents took! It became hard to believe that they had ever lived together. While my mother became paler and thinner in the intensity of her dedication to love, my father married fat rich Persephone, and, like her, became fat and rich. Having been frustrated in his desire to be Louisa, he turned to Persephone. His speech took on her turns of phrase. He constantly quoted her, as he had Louisa—in both cases he was unaware that he was doing so. He began to remember the tastes of extraordinary soups that his mother had made for him when he was a child, and Persephone researched the flavors. "Basically it was a borscht," he said, "but it had some special taste she added." Anxiously, "Do you think it could have been dill?" Persephone asked. ("Your grandmother Mrs. Wasserman, was the worst cook who ever lived," my mother has said to me. "That overdone meat, and watery canned vegetables. *Canned!*") They moved from Lombard Street to a massive house on Pacific Street, which a decorator made all white-on-white for them, and my father joined ("got into" is the phrase my mother used) the Concordia Club.

Why had Louisa ever married Michael, my father? That was the puzzle I had to consider, and all that any reach of my imagination could come up with was that after a lively and perhaps tiring adolescence (how unlike my own!) she wanted a rest.

. . .

My mother grew thinner over Bayard. Of course the affair did not go well: how could it, with Bayard controlling all the ammunition? Louisa had entirely changed over into a new role: she had gone from being the woman who is pursued to being the woman who waits. She stared often at the telephone, as though by magic she could evoke the clamorous ring that might announce his voice. With darkened eyes she stared at the door, which might open at his turn of the lock. Of course she had given him a key.

Bayard also shifted roles; he changed from being the pursuer to being the elusive one, who often did not phone, who was always late.

Louisa never rebuked him, or complained. Would he have liked it better if she had? Did he actually want a scold? Who knows—perhaps his wife would know. I am sure she has scolded for years, and there he is, still married to her.

Then one afternoon I came home and my mother was there in her pink robe, having cried a lot and saying that she had a cold, and after that there was no more Bayard, and I had missed the final scene.

She suffered terribly. Her pain was almost visible, so intensely was it present. It was nearly impossible for her to eat. She forced down a few boiled eggs, and sipped at milk and apologized (and apologized and apologized) for so frequently giving me TV dinners, and I could not convince her that I didn't mind.

Then my mother got really sick; her old colitis came back and she had to go to the hospital, for a month.

And so I went to stay with my father and Persephone, in the frilly white bedroom with its fourposter bed, "my" room. It was interesting there, and not quite what I had expected.

For one thing, I saw for the first time that Michael had not become Persephone; he was not just fat. He seemed lost in his fat, lost and a little wistful, sad. Not that he would have liked to have Louisa back; he was too sensible for that—but he struck me as a man who felt that he was missing out, or had missed out. "I really wonder if psychology was the field for me," he said. "Actually philosophy interests me considerably more. And, let's face it, a lot of my patients are basically shits. That's their basic problem."

(Loyal laughter from Persephone. Louisa would not have laughed.)

I also saw many qualities of my own in Michael, my non-Louisa qualities: his calm, his ambivalence, his fair complexion and long nose.

On most afternoons after school I stopped by the hospital to see my mother, who seemed slowly to be recovering both from Bayard and from her illness. As usual she was terribly worried about me, and as usual I tried to reassure her. I was fine. "Well, at least I don't have to worry about your being well fed," she remarked.

Louisa is not always charitable about Michael.

After my mother came home—and I, of course, with her—whenever the telephone rang she jumped violently, and she looked at me as though for protection from whatever it was going to say. But it was only Kate or one of her other friends, and she would tell them how she felt. I stayed in the living room while she was on the phone, until she forgot I was there, as she sat or paced and talked, and the long cord twisted and twitched out in the hall.

"It's really interesting how one can seem to be a

demanding shrew, or so I've been told," she said to Kate. "I would have thought I was quite what is called permissive. You know, it would be much easier for me if he were dead." And then she said, "And, aside from anything else, he has turned me into the most awful gloomy bore. I haven't said anything remotely funny for months," which was a little more like her old tone.

Once, in the middle of the night, the phone rang, very loud, just outside my mother's bedroom door. (She always brought it down the length of our hall when she went to bed.) Instantly awake, I knew that it was Bayard, and I was also sure that he was somewhere near, perhaps a little drunk. Wanting to come to see her. I was cold and afraid, and sure that she would let him; she would want another act to her drama.

Her voice surprised me, so wide awake, so *gay*. "Oh, Bayard, how nice. No, I wasn't asleep at all. In fact—well, no, that wouldn't be a good idea." She lowered her voice. "Someone's here. A friend." Then, louder and very cheerful, "Well, so nice to hear from you. Yes, you, too. Goodbye."

Amazing—talk about style!

But then, with the soft putting down of the receiver, she broke into horrible sobs that went on and on.

Well, at last, after many months, her pain seemed to go away, and she could even speak amusingly about that affair. "It must be a sort of initiation rite, the big affair with the married man," she said into the phone, to Kate. "The married man chosen for being very unlike your husband, and who turns out finally to be rather like your father. God, I really envy you, being out of such an impossible circle." She laughed, and sipped at her drink. "Well, I've got to go. Lewis is picking me up for dinner, and I want to feed Maude first."

It was much like her pre-Bayard conversations, but

there were subtle changes in my mother, visible perhaps only to one watching her intensely. She was slightly less open and enthusiastic than before, or perhaps her enthusiasms were more controlled. Her wit was more ironic than before Bayard. Of course these could be changes that occur with age; I had no way of knowing. But visibly her style of dress had changed: while before she had tended to somewhat subdued classics, to gray flannel and camel's hair, white wool and black cashmere, suddenly a lot of red entered her wardrobe: scarlet scarves and silk shirts and narrow velvet pants. She looked neat!

And she went back to her dinners with bachelors that sometimes turned into love affairs, and I went back to watching television, the beginnings of the Kennedys and listening to Dylan.

A year or so later, my grandmother Caroline died, and shortly after that it turned out that we were rich, or in any case much richer: Caroline had left everything to my mother. (Later it also turned out that Louisa's father, my grandfather Jack, had tried to contest her will! For that reason, and also because of a flare-up of colitis, she did not go back to the funeral.)

"What she did is terribly touching," my mother said to me, her eyes and her voice full of tears. "How terrible that I can't thank her—that we can't talk. We never did."

(I wondered: Is this a reason that she talks so much to me?)

And so my mother bought a small house for us, off Lake Street, next to the Presidio woods. She quit her job, and she fixed up the top floor of our new house (the house where Bayard had never been) as a studio for herself. She worked hard, and she began in a small way to be a success:

drawings in various galleries, a small show, a couple of short (but favorable) reviews.

Of course the money helped a lot, but I still think she showed some courage. I give my mother points for guts.

However, she made a couple of foolish mistakes —with me. In some excited burst, just after she got the money ("I'm adoring being *nouveau riche*," she said over the phone; she said it often), she asked me if I wanted to have my nose fixed. "I mean, if you'd rather have it a little smaller," she said.

"No, of course not."

"Well, I didn't mean—darling, of course I love the way you look." She laughed apologetically.

I laughed, too—forgivingly.

That suggestion was her first mistake, and of course her apologies are the second. She would like to apologize to me for all those years, and I have never worked out a way of telling her that watching her was a welcome change from TV for me—that in spite of everything, of Bayard and all her worries, she looked freer than anyone else in sight.

Nine / 1964

Andrew Chapin has the impression that his wife has just said something startling, but he is not sure; Sally's voice, as always, is so soft and gentle.

She repeats, "I think we have to get a divorce, Andrew."

It later occurred to Andrew that it was very like Sally to ask for a divorce at the breakfast table—not, as most wives would have done, he felt, in bed. He was not sure how he knew this about most wives. In any case, the neat breakfast table seemed the logical place for Sally's announcement. A non-intimate scene: both of them fully dressed, pink lipstick on Sally's delicate mouth, pale blue eye shadow on her lids: they are both outfitted for the day, for the outer world rather than for each other.

Then Sally says another startling thing: "I'm sorry, but I want to marry Alex."

"Alex—?"

She smiles a little at that; after all, they know only one Alex. Alex Magowan, who has been their close friend for

years; they have just nursed him through his own divorce
—or at least until now Andrew had assumed that the
nursing-through was a joint project.

"But Alex isn't really the point," Sally goes on, very
softly, very firmly. She has decided what to say. "My falling
in love with Alex was a symptom, not a cause. I mean, we
would have had to split up anyway."

"Really? Why?" Wanting more coffee, but feeling
that it would be a little tasteless to ask for it at just this
moment, instead Andrew leans back and looks at his wife, as
though trying to understand who she is. Her tired pale blue
eyes years ago held a haunted look that was, to Andrew,
terribly compelling. Her strong, rather prominent downy
chin. Darkening blond hair.

"You haven't noticed anything wrong?" she asks
softly.

The boys are off at school, but one of them has left a
transistor radio on; from somewhere blasts "I Want To Hold
Your Hand." Andrew and Sally exchange a look that
expresses one small area of agreement; they both hate the
Beatles.

"When?" Andrew asks.

"Oh, for the last few years. Or—I don't know, maybe
longer." Sally sighs. Then she bursts out, "You're so
Eastern—I've never felt at home with you. And all your rich
relatives, they're so polite to me." She begins to cry.

Torn between a desire to comfort her and a need to
satisfy intellectual curiosity, Andrew lets the latter win out.
"Why didn't you mention this fifteen years ago?"

"Oh, then I was so impressed. I thought marrying
you would make me part of all that. Part of your family."

"Christ, Sally, you are my family." Andrew is
quickly sorry to have said this. She cries harder, her mascara
runs. She had not planned to cry.

But just as Andrew pities her most it comes to him that Alex is from Seattle, and the corniness of this oppresses him. No one here but us real Westerners, he thinks. He says, "Alex is an excuse; he is not a symptom."

She stops crying, and in her reasonable voice she asks, "Well, what's worse?"

Looking at their familiar yellow-and-white Stranglware, a wedding present that is now only used for breakfast *à deux*, since most of it broke, Andrew begins to go into what is to be the first phase of his reaction to the divorce, which is disbelief. Can Sally have said what he had heard her say? Quite honestly he says to her, "I somehow don't believe this is us."

She narrows her eyes accusingly. "That just shows how little you noticed."

He won't let her get by with this. "I didn't notice that you and Alex were in love with each other, if that's what you mean. I thought we were all good friends."

She flushes, and pushes out that blond downed chin. "I didn't mean that. I meant between us." But before he can react to that she adds, in her clearest voice, "And I want you to know one thing: Alex and I haven't done—anything wrong. We've just talked."

For some reason this strikes Andrew as extremely funny. "You mean, you're telling me that you and Alex are madly in love and getting married without—without ever—." (He and Sally have no word for the act of love, which later strikes Andrew as a very bad sign.)

"What's so funny about that?" Sally says. Adding, cruelly, "It's what *we* did."

Half hearing her, Andrew goes on laughing, gasping, until he realizes that he is crying. Then, pretending to choke on his laughter, he rushes from the table to the downstairs bathroom, where he is sick.

. . .

The Magowan divorce, like an earthquake, sent tremors through their shocked circle of friends. The Magowans? Alex and *Grace?* Although for several years, since Allison has been sick, Grace had been behaving in a way that everyone thought was odd; she took Allison on long trips instead of to doctors, she spent most of her time alone with Allison.

Alex came over to tell Sally and Andrew about it. His normally florid face had a darker, unhealthy flush, as though his blood were infected. "I thought you people should be the first to know," he said, with no irony—in fact with considerable dignity. "Grace and I—we're breaking up."

As Alex said that, Andrew had an image of a ship, a wooden hull splitting apart in a storm, or tossed by a giant whale. And indeed the Magowans' marriage had the stately quality of a ship. They were majestic: they never did the messy things that other people sometimes did: no public spats, no drunken passes at others' mates. (Well, Andrew later thought, Sally and I didn't do too many of those things, either.)

Sally cried out, "Oh, no," and almost immediately began to cry.

Alex looked grimmer and darker still. One of his problems, which Andrew recognized but was helpless to alleviate, was that Alex had no vocabulary for the depth of what had happened to him. Even more than most people do, he spoke normally in clichés; things were terrific, or great, or really lousy. But how could you call a deserting wife or a mad child really lousy?

He spoke with a tremendous effort as his large hands gripped each other. "It's really this thing with Allison. God knows I'm no expert, but I seriously think the kid should see a psychiatrist."

"Of course she should," Andrew said gently.

Alex looked grateful. "Well, I'm afraid I said that a few too many times to Grace. God, it's like—like I'd insulted her. Like I'd told *her* to go to a psychiatrist. So now she wants to move back to New Hampshire with Allison. She thinks a small town is what Allison needs. God, I can't move to a small town in New Hampshire. I'm just getting started."

Allison by then was ten. She had more or less come out of an awful phase of not eating and of vomiting a lot. Now she got into fights. Seeming to have no notion of her own size, or sex, she physically attacked big boys, who sometimes hit her back. She was always in various forms of trouble at school. (A phase that preceded further withdrawal.) And Grace had never admitted any of this. "Oh, the kids are all fine," she would say.

Sally was speaking to Alex. "No, of course you couldn't move to New Hampshire," she said softly. And then, "Alex, would you like me to try to talk to Grace?"

"That's terrific of you, Sal. Really. But I just don't think so. She's become—unreasonable."

"Okay. But if there's anything we can do. . ."

And so Grace left town with Allison, leaving Alex with the two other children, Douglas and Jennifer. And the two somewhat diminished families became closer than ever. Sally made Christmas and Thanksgiving dinners for all of them. Alex, who was getting quickly rich in housing developments, sometimes took them all out lavishly, to family dinners at the Palace Hotel, or the Redwood Room at the Clift.

Once at the St. Francis, in a bar adjoining the dining room, they saw someone they all thought they knew: Louisa Wasserman. Whoever it was, she was totally absorbed in a huge red-haired man. Impressive. And Louisa, or whoever, did not see them, or perhaps she pretended not to. (And

Sally had the further—curious—impression that Andrew did not want to see Louisa.)

"If that's Louisa, she really looks terrific," Sally said, looking at Andrew. "I heard she and Michael got a divorce."

"One more." Alex scowled. Then he smiled at his friends. "I hope you people realize how lucky you are."

They thought they did.

And so, after several more painful conversations, and more tears, Andrew moves into a bachelor pad on Telegraph Hill, with a king-sized bed and an expensive view of the city, a long way across town from the Pacific Heights where Sally and the boys remain. He has two bedrooms, one that is equipped for weekend visits with bunk beds—those ex-family rituals that by the sixties are such a commonplace. Andrew sees his life as moving into realms of situation comedy. It makes him cringe, the banality of it all. For Andrew has always had an almost artistic double vision of himself—the "almost" keeps him a professor rather than an artist.

(In fact during these personally lively years, he almost stops thinking about writing.)

By day he teaches his classes, and at night he stays at home with his guilts. (Guilt was the phase that succeeded surprise, that preceded rage.) Trying to read, staring across the spangled city, he considers his failures as a husband. He wanted her to read all his books. He insisted on making love even when she was tired or had a bad cold. He did not teach the boys to play baseball. He talked too much. "You filled up all the space," Sally has said, in one of those penultimate conversations. "There was no room for me." And so she is marrying silent Alex, the Westerner.

Andrew drinks too much.

One night, in the midst of his second brandy, Alex telephones. He sounds very like himself. "I—uh —wondered if perhaps we shouldn't get together, talk a few things over."

"Why?" Andrew realizes instantly that he does not in the least want to see Alex, or to talk things over.

"Well—uh—if that's how you feel—."

"Alexander, I just don't see the point. What's to say?"

"Well—uh—no hard feelings."

"Well, perhaps a few." Andrew hangs up, and thinks: You stupid bastard, I have plenty of hard feelings. And a not startling but new insight occurs to him: Alex speaks so tritely because his mind is trite. Alex is basically an ass.

Then he begins to be angry at Sally. The ungrateful bitch.

There is a period of voluptuous fantasies, a period during which, with liberated eyes, a freed libido, he observes all his girl students—in fact all girls. And here again, new cause for anger at Sally: he has been such a faithful husband that he has almost never thought of his students "in that way"—despite all the enticing literature on the subject, the proliferation of good-to-bad novels and stories on student-professor affairs.

For instance, Miss James, in the front row of his American Literature course. Miss Isabel James. Her name delights him; he hopes that none of her friends call her Iz. She has pale blue eyes and darkening blond hair, and small pretty legs. He has never allowed himself to think for long about Miss James. But now, why not?

Jill turns out to be why not, picking him up in City Lights Book Store, in front of Poetry. "Mister, would you mind driving me home? I've been celebrating a suicide and I really feel rotten."

A preposterous request, and so he asks, "Where do you live?"

"Potrero. Really—thanks."

As though he had said yes, she starts across the basement floor, and so he follows her. He notices then that her feet are bare and that she is extremely fat. She pauses at the counter upstairs to pay for a thick paperback called Erections, Ejaculations, Exhibitions, and Other Tales of Ordinary Madness. Christ, where is he?

She and the thin black who takes her money discuss the book.

"Bukowski. Yeah, wow."

"I really dig him. *Really.*"

"Did you hear about Bill?"

"Yeah, too bad. They find his body?"

"Not yet."

"Too bad. I wonder what happened to his paintings."

"He'd burned them all."

"Wow."

Her feet are rather small for such a big girl, and delicately arched. Dirty, of course, on the soles, with the dirt seeping upward, up the slightly calloused pink sides. Spiky blondish hairs stand out from the sides of her legs. Observing this last, Andrew thinks of two separate things simultaneously: the hairs remind him of the here-and-there spiky down on Sally's chin, and he wonders if this girl shaves under her arms. The idea that she might not is suddenly erotic.

Following her out to the sidewalk, he is very aware of how they must look. Himself middle-aged, dark, trim, a man handsome in a not quite usual way, in conventional clothes: old tweed jacket, turtleneck, gray flannels. And this big blond barefoot girl, who looks dirty and exhausted. Does anyone imagine her to be his daughter? Does everyone think they are going off somewhere to make love?

Is that what they are going to do?

Across Columbus Avenue, at the Broadway intersection, hawkers announce the garish start of the topless era. Big live breasts! Real ones! On girls, all kinds of girls. Even college girls. There is a place that specializes in college girls. Folks—step right up? Andrew has the quick and absurd fantasy that he does step right up and finds, in the college-girl place, Miss Isabel James. Topless. But he is with another girl.

"I'm Jill," the girl says, settling back in his car. "Say, this is really nice of you. I wouldn't have asked but this afternoon a friend of mine—I guess a former friend —jumped off the Golden Gate Bridge. Do many people jump off the Bay, do you know? He wasn't anyone I liked any more, but it upsets me when someone dies that I ever made it with. It makes me feel a little dead. Does that make any sense? You'd better turn left at the next light."

She talks almost all the way to her house on Potrero Hill, and by the time they get there Andrew has heard a lot of crazy stuff. She used to make it with her brother, as she puts it. George. In fact she also has several friends named George. She grew up in Hollywood, and she has reason to believe that George, or someone named George, was or is also making it with her stepmother, or is it her mother? George has this curious quirk: he likes to do it standing up, and really best in a shower.

She is much too crazy; never mind what she does under her arms.

Outside her house, still in the car, he says good night to her. He asks her, "Are you okay now?"

"Yes, but come on in. I've got sort of a nice place."

And so, again, he follows her.

Into a small low house, which, when she switches on a light, appears to be entirely inhabited by ferns and some other indistinguishable fernlike plants. Everywhere rows of small wrinkled or curly leaves, a feathery profusion of fronds. Andrew is somehow touched: how she must care for her plants! (He is later to see her make slow gestures over them, blessing them, saying good night.)

Now she turns to Andrew. Reaching, she takes his face in her small firm hands. She takes his mouth with hers.

"I'm very square; I really like to do it best in bed, do you? Come on, put your clothes over there. Do you want the light off? Take it easy; we have all night, at least, don't we? You're not married or shacked up or anything? Do you like me to kiss you there?"

By the time Jill has said all that, they are in bed, and Andrew is discovering the firmness of all that flesh, how smooth she is, and her sweet clean unexpected smell of baby powder.

Propped on an elbow, she later says, "You know, this isn't a criticism or anything, but when you kiss me here if you'd touch me there at the same time I'd really like it." Taking his hand, she illustrates, and then she says, "Poor Bill—the guy who committed suicide. I honestly think he hated sex, another person's body. God knows he liked his own, but he didn't have the guts to be a fag. Always wanting to be kissed, giving it to me like some kind of prize. An honor. But it really is interesting, isn't it, the different things different people like to do. I'm absolutely fascinated."

Andrew sleepily agrees that he is, too. He is glad she could not know how few girls actually, he had any experience of—merely a handful of college affairs, then years of Sally.

"Would you like to do it again? Well, I guess you would. You know, you're really cool."

That night, waking in some small hour next to Jill, Andrew experiences a kind of delusion, almost hallucinatory in its intensity—and it is only the first in a series of identical delusions. Simply, he believes that Jill is Sally. He is sufficiently awake to know that this is not true—he knows who Jill is, more or less—but the message that his flesh receives is a message from Sally's sleeping flesh, dry flesh, so dissimilar to Jill's. It is almost as though Jill were somehow inhabited by Sally. Or perhaps as though he were.

Then, and relevantly, he remembers that often in dreams he still lives in his parents' house, the Long Island home of his boyhood; in dreams he spends rainy afternoons on the glassed-in veranda, watching the lashing gray Atlantic. In dreams he still quarrels with his parents, at their formal dinner table.

In the morning he and Jill make love again and then from the bed he watches her beneficent gestures over her ferns, and he feels great tenderness for this fat, improbable, and generous girl.

At breakfast (delicious eggs, tasting mysteriously of curry and onions and cream cheese and sherry) she tells him more of her experiences, all sexual, some fairly bizarre.

Andrew observes his own reactions curiously; this is a conversation that normally he would find unattractive. But he finds this one simply interesting, and often very funny.

Jill's attitude (he thinks), despite an impressive bulk of experience, is childlike still; she is never worldly or weary about it all. (Only much later does he wonder how much of what she said was true.)

Nor, strangely, does it then occur to Andrew to wonder what she would find to say about him. He is too replete, too proud. He asks, "Can I see you tonight?"

"Oh? Well, sure."

Partly because he is used to monogamy, Andrew falls into a pattern of seeing Jill every night, or almost every night. They do not see each other on the weekends when he has the boys. If you sleep with someone, you sleep with them every night, he not quite consciously thinks.

He brings food and wine and sometimes flowers—he knows flowers are superfluous in that ferny bower, but he likes to bring flowers to a girl—and together they cook and eat and make love among the ferns, in that small hillside house. A pleasant pattern—it resembles love.

Andrew (the professor) examines cautiously what it is that he does feel for Jill, and finds affection, gratitude, occasional irritation. She reads only crazy books, she is messy, she would much rather discuss sex than politics. (Politics?) He likes her, and he doesn't like her, and he loves her in bed. As simple, as complicated as that.

But one thing that (then) very much pleases Andrew about Jill is what he feels to be the originality of his choice of her—in fact the originality of Jill. So much about his life, especially the episodes surrounding his divorce, has struck him as trite, as more banal than tragic, or even sad: Sally's announcement at breakfast, and so on, up to and very much including the wooden phone call from Alex Magowan. It is also trite that he is now with a much younger woman. But not Jill. She is as far as possible from the stereotype, the Bunny. He is grateful for her dirty feet and her fat, her eccentric ferns and her crazy conversation.

. . .

But again and again in his dreams he is married to Sally. It is neither terrible nor marvelous: they are simply married. For good.

One night at dinner, a Monday night, Jill is talking about her brother George, who is back in town. She mentions his shower fixation. "He's sort of a fanatic," Jill says. "But good."

"He must be terribly clean."

But as she goes on a single fact slowly and surely intrudes on Andrew's love- and wine-happy mind: she is not discussing the past; she is talking about what she and George did on the weekend immediately past, and almost certainly in this very room. Andrew looks at the rumpled bed from which they have just arisen.

Tightly he asks her, "You spent a lot of time with George last weekend?"

Of course his tone makes her defensive, and she tightly answers, "Yes."

They both know exactly what has just been said, and they sit together in a silence that is like smog, heavy and oppressive and hard to breathe.

It is Jill who breaks into it. "Look, do I ever ask you anything? How do I know what you do on weekends with your wife?"

"I don't see her on weekends, just the boys. Besides, she's not my wife."

But she has touched a nerve. He has had fantasies of making love to Sally again, and, cruelly, in the fantasies she is always the slender haunted girl he has just married, Sally warm with delight; she is not his dry exhausted wife, speaking of headaches in a voice he can hardly hear.

He has, of course, had fantasies of Alex with Sally.

"She's not my wife—we're divorced," he repeats, out of varieties of anger and frustration.

Jill has warmed to another issue. "Besides, I really don't see this fidelity bit. I never have. Why do people have to own each other? Sex is the way I communicate with people. Why should I only talk to one person?"

He has no answers.

"Who do I hurt by being with a lot of guys? What's *bad?*"

What she says is absolutely true; she is not hurting anyone. Except possibly Andrew, and he can fasten onto no right that he has over her, not even the right to be hurt.

Very gently she says to him, "You're not quite ready for that, are you? Don't feel bad, a lot of guys aren't."

Very confused, but dimly aware that he is being dismissed, Andrew stands up to go.

"Call me," Jill says—very friendly. "I'd really like to see you sometime."

Andrew does not call Jill. He thinks about her instead, and finally he realizes that not seeing her is, curiously, a relief to him.

He begins to think again about Miss Isabel James, who is not registered for classes this quarter. It occurs to him that she might be in the phone book, and she is—she even lives nearby, on Russian Hill.

Of course she remembers him. Dr. Chapin; in fact they fall in love with each other and within a short time they marry. Isabel James Chapin.

Andrew rarely thinks of Jill, the post-beatnik, early flower and fern girl. However, a few years later, during a time when much is written and said about "hippies," with a certain disappointment Andrew recognizes Jill in every paragraph; he sees her vaunted freedom as programmatic —and thus he is able to dismiss her from his mind, for good.

But, married to Isabel, living in a new house in Sausalito, he dreams still that he is married to Sally. And he lives in his parents' old house on the distant Atlantic.

And, inexorably, he and Isabel have three children, three more boys. At some point it occurs to Andrew's quirky mind that he is producing sons instead of literature—as, often, women are said to do.

But this bothers him less and less.

Ten / 1966

Flowering privet still surrounds the pool, where so long ago Louisa and Kate arranged themselves in those poses (sex appeal!) and where, on a May afternoon, they both now sit. An afternoon a few days after Jack Calloway's funeral. (Curiously, since they could not have been described as *close*, Jack and Caroline died within three years of each other. And, further irony: Jack died of lung cancer, having for years fought "rumors" linking tobacco and harm to the lungs.) Louisa has come for the funeral, and to settle possessions.

And Kate has come in time to visit her old friend —just not in time for Jack's funeral; she never liked Jack at all. This is her vacation from her Berkeley family; after leaving Louisa she will go on to see her own parents, Jane and Charles Flickinger, who are still alive, in New Jersey.

Although Louisa came for her father's funeral, what has happened has been something astounding: she has remet and fallen in love with John Jeffreys—John from her (and Kate's) early past. It is as though John were the true purpose of her trip—in fact that is how she comes to see it.

. . .

Standing near her father's grave, looking out into a crowd of familiar and half-familiar faces, she is caught by a pair of dark, pained, and intelligent eyes that have sought her eyes. John Jeffreys. (But with white, white hair. He is very striking.) Before looking down (she feels that she must not stare, not here) she is struck with a curious thought: she thinks, He knows everything about me.

That night, having contrived to be alone (with difficulty; everyone means so well), Louisa responds to a knock at the door.

John says, "You don't mind?" Serious, tentative.

"No, of course not. Come in. You can be my excuse for having a drink."

(These are two very Southern people.)

They have drinks, they talk without saying very much. Then Louisa says, "God, what a hot night! Why don't we have a swim?"

"Great."

As simply as that they leave the house; they walk across the lawn, past looming abandoned stables and the huge formally trimmed boxwood.

At the edge of the pool, not quite looking at each other, they take off their clothes; they slip slowly into the cool receiving water. They swim around, they exclaim, "It feels marvelous!"

They get out.

Naked, in the warm black night, in the sweet smells of privet and of spring itself, they turn toward each other. They kiss, they begin to touch each other's smooth and supple skin.

They have fallen in love.

. . .

But for a while it seems to Louisa that what has happened between them is symbolic, rather than actual —that "Louisa" and "John," of a certain time and place, are "in love." It is at first too easy, even too appropriate. What is needed is a melting down, a diffusing of all the elements involved, and eventually that, too, takes place.

(Just as, some years later, when Louisa and John, very high on grass, make love, she has the sense of watching two puppets, two white stick figures, who are making love—all of whose violent sensations she herself experiences. And later she tries, and fails, to draw those figures.)

Now Louisa's conversation leaps about, as she tries to explain to her old friend all the recent and violent events of her life, there on the familiar edge of the pool.

The two women's bodies have changed with age (of course) and in opposite directions: Kate's is fuller, softer, whereas Louisa's has hardened; she is bony, perhaps too thin.

"Well?" Louisa asks, as though continuing a logical sequence, which she is not. "How *should* I feel—could I feel? He did behave so badly, really dishonestly." She is speaking, Kate understands, of Jack, her father, and his attempt to contest her mother's will, in which Caroline left all her money to Louisa.

"What's strange, in a way," she continues, with her own illogic (which makes sense to Kate), "is that I feel as though I'd come to my mother's funeral. To bury Caroline. In fact during the service that's what I was thinking, that it was Caroline in the coffin. In the earth." A pause. Then, "You know, when she actually died I was still in mourning for Bayard. Not to mention laid up with colitis. I somehow missed her death."

Louisa goes on in this vein, saying things that Kate half knows. Kate listens loyally, but her mind is not there. She is thinking about her husband, David, the great heart surgeon. Thinking: *Is* David fucking that nurse, that blond Miss Murray? Angrily, painfully, she thinks: Stupid prick, how trite of him. David at forty-five. The male menopause. Can I help being fat? Well, yes, I could help it, but screw him, why should I?

"I am literally stricken with her loss," Louisa says, still speaking of her mother. "And then John," she says, now unstricken, and she smiles deeply, an inward, pervasive smile.

John has just moved back to Virginia, after an unfortunate life in New York: a dead wife, a patchy career. (This reinforces the local view that it is dangerous to marry Yankees, and to try to work up there. Just look at that Calloway girl, that poor Louisa.) Aware of this view, John and Louisa think, and they say to each other: "They don't know the half of it."

To Kate, John is still a vivid memory of early pain, turning her down. ("Shall we take our clothes off, John—and do everything?" "You don't know what you're talking about.") And then dumping her for that girl, that dumb little bitch, that—? (No, not Miss Murray.) She asks Louisa, "What was that girl's name, do you remember? The one John liked for a while, after me?" She gives that last phrase a wry twist.

"Mary Beth Williamson." Louisa has an odd memory. She laughs. "John couldn't remember her name, either. God, what a dumb little bitch she was."

"He doesn't?" Then maybe in twenty years David won't remember the nurse's name, but by then it will be too late. Or—maybe he isn't screwing her after all. "It's so hot," Kate says, and she flops flatly into the pool, a large lazy splash.

Feeling her friend's unhappiness (What is wrong with Kate? She doesn't say), Louisa is dimly reminded of another time, of herself excited and "in love," at a time of sadness for Kate. And she remembers that she was in love with Richard Trowbridge (Richard *Trow*bridge?) and Kate was mourning over John. Snow, and sledding on the golf course. She remembers everything.

And now she loves John, and she is also mourning. In her strange, exaggerated state of mind, she could easily cry or laugh. In fact she does a lot of both. Now she slips into the pool after Kate. In tandem, more or less, they swim around its out-of-style kidney shape. They get out together.

A new thought bursts from Louisa, this time a funny one. "Kate, did I tell you what happened to Richard Trowbridge? John just told me last night." (She loves to say John's name.)

"Richard—?"

"You remember Richard. He was mad about you, and then me." Louisa begins to laugh.

Kate has remembered. "Oh, Richard."

"Well, he's living in Washington, and he's in the C.I.A.! He's important there!" Louisa chokes on this.

"The C.I.A.—that's marvelous." Kate laughs, too; for various (and divergent) reasons they are both almost hysterical.

"The C.I.A.—"

"Richard—"

"How perfect—"

"Our country really needs—"

But (and again for separate reasons) neither of them can laugh long, and they sober up together. Kate says, "I don't know, I really wonder about marriage."

"Oh?"

Kate gestures, unspecifically. "Fifteen years—it's so long. It's so easy to get out of touch."

"Touch" makes Louisa think of John. His touch. But she tries to listen. "Out of touch?"

"You sort of stop talking. I mean, of course we still talk, but a lot of it is about the kids. Lists for a Christmas party. Income tax. You know."

"I.can't imagine fifteen years," Louisa says, not very helpfully. But the very idea has made her vulnerable spirits sink. Where will they be, she and John, in fifteen years? *Should* they marry?

And you almost stop screwing. Kate goes on to herself, except for an occasional quick morning bout. David waking up with a hard-on, happening to be next to me. Not like years past, when we waited for the kids to go to sleep so we could do it on the sofa, listening to Ella, or Frank —hoping the music drowned us out.

Not only the contents of her mind but the impossibility of speaking them is oppressive to Kate; she feels lonely, and isolated from Louisa, who seemingly is saying everything in *her* mind. And Kate wonders: Do I not tell Louisa about what is nearly ruining me with worry out of pride, what is called false pride? Or don't I say it because saying it might make it worse, like not screaming during physical pain. ("I'm afraid David is fucking his nurse" would be a scream.) Kate doesn't know. she never cried out during the difficult births of her children. Stephen, Jane, Louisa, and Christopher, who is only three, who was not exactly intended. (But should she have cried out?)

"Christ," Kate says, instead of saying anything else, "I've got to take off some weight."

"Oh, why? There're so many skinny women around. I love the way you look," Louisa ardently tells her.

Kate laughs. "You're crazy." But of course she is pleased.

"So—what else is new?"

Louisa says, "I suppose you don't remember that time you came to see me and Michael? When I was pregnant?"

"Of course I do. You lived in a funny sort of rented house, and after dinner those other people came over. The boy who took me to lunch that time."

"Andrew Chapin. That's funny—he reminds me of John. Do you think they're a type?"

"Perhaps." Sighing, Kate looks down at her legs, foreshortened in the water, pale and fat-looking. But is Louisa right, or just being nice? Is it okay to be fat?

Louisa is saying, "But you were so marvelous that time; that's what I remember. You really lit into Michael about my having a terrible full-time job so that he could go to graduate school."

"Did I? What a guest!"

"But you were right. Why should I have been the one? And what's awful is that at the time it seemed perfectly normal. And I was so crazy that I thought Michael was normal."

"I don't really remember that part of it." (I was too absorbed in missing David, Kate remembers.)

For many reasons Kate would like not to see John Jeffreys on this brief visit, and so far she has not. She does not want to see John himself, or John and Louisa, "in love."

But this is unavoidable; it is a small town still, and there they all are.

A party is given for Louisa, a small quiet one, since there has just been a funeral, and of course it is known that Kate is visiting there, is staying at the Inn. She has persuaded Louisa that she needs some time alone, not saying just why. "At this point the utmost luxury that I can imagine is an anonymous hotel," which the Inn is not, but she makes do there.

And everyone remembers the girlhood of Louisa and Kate. ("That cute little red-haired Yankee girl—whatever happened to her people?") Dashing young Kate, wearing red, who came down and broke the hearts of several Southern boys: Richard Trowbridge (but then he got to like Louisa, and she ditched him), and then John Jeffreys. So now the chivalrous story goes: Southern boys do not ditch girls.

As all her life she has, undecorous, unrestrained Kate admires the decorum and restraint of Southerners; even Louisa has a curious tendency to behave well at times when Kate might not. These gentle old people sip tall drinks of bourbon and water. (Mint juleps are too much trouble, and are locally regarded as a little pretentious, a drink that rich Yankees might serve—that Kate's parents often did serve, until they caught on that it was not the thing to do.) Gentle references are made to Louisa's dead parents, and to the recent funeral. "I did think the service went well, didn't you, Louisa, dear? And the flowers were lovely. The perfect time of year."

(Kate wants to say, "How very considerate of Jack to die in May." Or a part of her wants to say that. Another part would like to be as gentle as these people are.)

And Louisa. She is wearing such a Southern dress. Pale blue, with tiny flowers of a deeper blue, a tucked bodice, flowing skirt. (Miss Louisa.) Her hazel eyes are enormous, tearing readily at the names of her parents. Tearing at the sight or voice of John, whom she is for the moment passing off as a kind old friend. "John has been such a help." She even says that, as Kate thinks: Christ!

John Jeffreys. It is apparent to Kate that at first he does not know who she is (she was such a slender girl, back then) and so she is free to watch him. He is still very thin, but with startlingly white hair, so that his eyes are even larger and darker than they were. But the same eyes. Same sad witty intelligent face. Kate has, of course, been filled in on his life by Louisa. His wife's suicide, his attempts at careers. Drinking too much. Playing the piano. In everything John is always somewhat tentative, not quite committed—Kate is suddenly aware of this, and of the fact that he hasn't changed at all; he is as Southern, as gracefully elusive, as when he was a boy, and Kate experiences a twist of fear for Louisa. (But why? Louisa has always, somehow, managed to survive: Louisa is a born survivor.)

"Your father would have liked—"

"Remember the time that Jack—?"

"Caroline—"

"A perfect time—"

So those fading voices continue, over cool chicken salad and hot biscuits and tomatoes (from someone's garden) and iced tea—so gentle and so false—until Kate is choking on an interior scream that threatens to climb into her throat, to explode in her mouth. *Jack Calloway was a terrible person, a noisy bigot, screwing everything he could, including my mother. Do any of you remember Jane Flickinger, that chic Midwestern lady, that sucker for Southern charm? Screwed everyone and always made sure that Caroline knew. He reduced his wife to a dry shadow, and*

*did what he could to wreck his daughter, but Louisa somehow finally
evaded him. She survives.*

Of course she says nothing at all.

John Jeffreys has recognized her; he is standing at her
elbow, lightly smiling. They exchange sounds of recognition, and greetings. He says, "Such intensity in your eyes.
I'm sure you won't tell me any thoughts."

So Kate says, "You watch out, or I *will* tell you some
of my thoughts." The old Kate: challenging, emphatic.

He smiles. "Will you if I get you a drink?"

She smiles, too, managing an almost Southern,
guarded smile, and yields her glass. As, cruelly, she thinks
that he is a perfect husband for rich women. And then she
hates herself for having thought that—it isn't *true*.

By now it is late, past dinner. The pale firefly dusk
has been replaced by a dark blue night sky, across which
there are billowing white clouds. This particular house is out
in the country, in the hills beyond the town; the sky is huge.

Kate has a sudden and strong sense of being drunk.
Odd: normally she can drink quite a lot, but now she feels a
slow lurch within her head as John comes up with another,
stronger drink.

She tells him, "Christ, I really feel drunk." He used
to hate her swearing, she remembers, but now his face looks
only concerned, and kind.

"Really?" he asks. "Do you want to go home?"

"I probably should. I might start being a disgrace."

He smiles, and goes over to Louisa, who (for decorum) has come in her own car. In Jack's latest (last) Mer-
cedes. And so it is arranged. John will drive Kate back to the
Inn.

They speak farewells to their hosts, who seem to
remember something, seeing Kate and John together; as

though struck by some distant echo, those old faces are momentarily alight with recognition.

During the round of farewells, Kate has finished her new drink, which has made her feel much worse.

"I'm really sorry," she says to John in the car, his shabby old Ford. "I'm really not in terribly good shape."

The billowing clouds are enormous, very white against the midnight blue. It is somehow an unreal sky. Unnatural.

"Do you want to talk?" asks John. "We are old friends." He says this with the gentlest irony.

Christ! It makes her cry.

She says, "I think my husband—David—is fucking his nurse." She has blurted this out; she is out of control. A noisy Yankee. Drunk.

"But is it important?" His gentle voice.

"Of course it's important. Christ, what do you mean?"

"I just asked. I meant important to David. It might not be, you know."

He has stopped the car, off from the country road, in a grove of pines. He sighs. (He has just realized that he is trying to rescue yet another woman.)

Kate turns to him; she is aware suddenly and vividly of the sexiness of their situation, and of the significance of what he has just said.

She murmurs, "It might be something unimportant to David?"

"Yes, very unimportant." But they are no longer talking about David.

They reach for each other; they begin to kiss, to cling together.

But Kate is sick. Nausea rises in her throat, a quick

wave, so that she swallows hard. She breaks from John; she opens the door and leans out. She vomits, convulsively.

When she is through, drained and exhausted, she closes the door, leans back on the seat. John hands her a handkerchief.

They are both quiet, and then Kate bursts out, "God, what were we doing?"

"Maybe something unimportant."

"But Louisa—David—"

"They aren't here. And you're a really attractive woman. You always have been."

"John, please don't give me that Southern shit. Not just now."

He laughs.

He starts the car; he drives her into town, to the Inn. And that is that, except that it is an incident to which Kate gives a lot of thought.

She begins, of course, by supposing that they had gone on, had completed the act so impetuously begun, or perhaps the act begun twenty years ago, which could have been another thing that John meant to say. Okay: they have made love, fucked, in a parked car on a country road, in a grove of pines. Two old friends. What did it mean? That John did not really love Louisa? No, but it would mean exactly that to Louisa if John were foolish (or cruel) enough to tell her. (If John were Jack Calloway.) And she remembers what she has not thought of for years: that boy, that Andrew Chapin. Suppose they had gone on to a motel, as they both had wanted to do?

David of course has denied screwing the nurse, screwing any nurse, and now Kate thinks of him with a sort of tired affection, bringing tears to her eyes for a moment.

"Do you think John has changed a lot?" Louisa asks. It is her way of asking, "What do you think of John? Isn't he marvelous?"

Being "in love" has made Louisa younger; she laughs a lot and finds it hard to concentrate on anything but John.

"I don't know." Dishearteningly, Kate realizes that whatever she says will not matter much. However, she tries. "The trouble is that it's hard to separate John now from John then. Old images impinge," she says.

"Exactly!" Louisa seizes on this. "I sometimes wonder who I'm in love with. I mean, it must be at least partially the boy we knew all that time ago—"

"He looks a lot the same. Thin. But that marvelous hair."

"Yes, I'd have known him anywhere," Louisa breathes. Then, with the jumpiness that presently characterizes her conversation, "I'm so worried about Maude," she says. "All the summer-of-love flower-child stuff that we keep reading about. She writes, but all she says is that things are 'really beautiful.'"

"Well, maybe they are?"

Louisa frowns, then grins. "In any case she's happier. She did used to be so lonely. Isolated. And hunched over those enormous breasts. Of course I would have a daughter with huge breasts." She laughs.

Kate says, remembering, "I think Stephen said he saw her somewhere. He said she looked great. Wouldn't it be great if they were friends?"

At her own insistence Kate goes for long walks alone, around the town and out a little way into the surrounding countryside. Purposefully (sentimentally) she chooses the directions that she used to take with John, that spring. She takes roads leading out of town and into the woods, the pine-needled paths, in the sunny, piny air. But the paths have gone wrong—or something has.

She comes to the top of a hill (a place where she and John used to stop and kiss, or so she now believes). From there you could see an ancient cornfield, overgrown in springtime with wild flowers, and after the field a thick growth of green, lining the creek. And somewhere down there was a small romantic road, a cart track, actually; two people coming down from the woods in single file could walk there together, holding hands above the wild grasses, the tiny flowers that filled the ruts.

But now: Kate looks down a red clay bank, steeply slashed into the hillside. A highway, a superhighway. A subdivision of "Colonial" white bungalows.

Christ, have they buried the creek?

"Christ, did they bury the creek?" Kate asks this of Louisa, at dinner in what is now Louisa's house. (It is curious that after contesting his wife's will, contesting Louisa's inheritance from her mother, Jack has still left her almost everything. Perhaps he thought that otherwise it would not look well.) Louisa and Kate and John—they are being served by a black woman whom Louisa has introduced as Mary, who looks very much like the maid the Calloways had a long time ago (twenty-five years?), when Louisa and Kate first met.

John smiles, and Kate wonders. Could he be remembering their walks? Does he know where she went that afternoon and what was in her mind? Probably, she decides.

He says, "The creek might as well have been buried. That subdivision."

The dining room is at the end of a wing, in that sprawling, oversized house. There are windows on three sides, long windows, and now light from their bright table falls outside on slick rhododendron leaves, the bushes grown enormous, bearing heavy, creamy blooms. Kate remembers how awed she was by that room, years back: the imposing windows, so much bright crystal and silver. The several maids, at times a butler. A romantic room—Kate thinks that Louisa and John should be here alone.

But, after all, she is leaving the next day, and they insisted that she come.

She feels that she and John have put away whatever happened and did not happen a few nights ago; it was unimportant. He kissed her and she threw up.

In her exaggerated way Kate complains, "I don't know where anything is! I'm lost."

Affectionately Louisa laughs. "It is confusing."

"I went by our old house—you know, where we used to live," Kate tells them. "And it was so strange. I stood there staring at the house, and I got no message from it at all."

Of course they have understood her.

"Perhaps it's changed?"

"Too many other people?"

Kate agrees. "But it's just as well," she says. "I might have cried." and then, "Louisa, you wouldn't believe it, but I had trouble getting back from there to here—how many thousand times—"

At this both women's eyes tear over for a minute; but then at another memory Kate begins to laugh. She asks, "Do you remember one morning we were riding to school on our bikes, and you told me you'd written a song the night before, and you sang it for me?"

"Sort of—"

"You know what it was? 'Stardust.' "

Louisa laughs. "You hadn't heard it?"

"No. What a terrible bitch you were."

. . .

Later in the evening they are sitting in the living room, that baronial walnut-and-velvet non-intimate room. But the three of them have made an intimate corner for themselves, three deep chairs pulled together near the fireplace—where, instead of a fire, on the cool clean stones (those expensive slabs of granite from Vermont) Louisa has placed a lavish basket of roses from the garden. Petals of every shade, yellow to orange to vermilion. The scent of roses wafts to where they sit, and contributes, perhaps, to the sentimental mood that has settled on the group. (Though, after all, they are old friends.)

They are drinking tall Southern drinks: bourbon with ice and a lot of water.

Each of them has special obsessions:

Louisa would like to say how it feels when parents die, and in the saying perhaps she will find out. On and off all evening she has been attempting this. "There's a curious near-exhilaration," she says excitedly. "A release. Of course along with other feelings, loss and anger. All that. But I have this odd sense of being freer now—I don't mean just the money. Free to do things. The truth is," she tells them seriously, "I might draw better now. Am I making any sense at all?"

"Of course you are," they tell her, and John adds, "That's probably how people should feel all the time." His voice is both dry and wistful. He is a man who has never been "released." His talents and most of his feelings, except at moments, remain permanently locked.

In the shadowed room, the lamplit corner, all three people look very young, although possibly Louisa and John have this look because they are "in love."

Kate is getting drunk—again. The drink makes her

perspective maudlin as she looks at her two old friends, who are not really young at all, who have fallen in love late in life. At the moment this touches Kate with sadness, this late love—as though she were the only person who knew how old they are. (A not untrue perception: Louisa and John have indeed forgotten their ages.)

And then she has an even more maudlin thought (or is it that?), a wish for her husband, for David. She thinks, or hopes: I hope you were screwing that nurse. I hope she was lovely and generous and that you had a great time.

Later she is to remember thinking this, with a sort of outraged amazement: Christ, even for a moment, how could she have wished that, even for David? But later still she will come back to it, and will decide that though she could not be that giving for long, that is how she should be all the time. How people should be.

(They have all been quiet for a while.)

John is experiencing a familiar sort of sadness, like sea fog, a brume at the edges of his mind. A heaviness, a dimness where there should be light. *What does it matter whose money it is?* He knows that that is how to feel; Louisa doesn't care. But she has her work; she is moderately successful in her work—she didn't need to inherit money. He needed to and did not, which would seem to be the way of the world. And he knows himself to be a rescuer of women—he can't help it. This worries him; if once she needed to be rescued, now Louisa has apparently rescued herself. He is not sure that she needs him—or does *that* matter, any more than the money does?

The next day, which is Kate's last in town, Louisa picks her up at the Inn and brings her home for a morning swim. They lounge about, as always, or almost so: the pressure of time, a plane to be caught, makes them both more cryptic than usual, and a little tense. Old friends, they are trying to say a lot in a short time—knowing that they will see each other soon, in California, but also aware that this place, this pool, is their scene of intimacy.

And they are both hung over, especially Kate. But from inside her painful head she decides that it is important to be honest with her friend.

"I'm sorry if I've been a depressed guest," she says, "but I've been worrying about David."

"Oh?"

"I think he's screwing his nurse."

"*Really?*" (As she says this, Louisa suddenly realizes that she has never been fond of David—and how odd that she did not notice this lack of affection before.)

"I'm pretty sure. Funny excuses about being late for dinner. Coming home a little gassed. He's a rotten liar."

"Oh, Kate—"

"Well, I suppose that beats admitting it? And surgeons are odd about sex, they really are."

"God, that's too bad." (David is a cold person, Louisa is thinking. *Why* should Kate be married to him?)

Silently they sit there, legs dangling in the warm greenish water, in the once-fashionable shape of the big white pool.

"It could be unimportant," muses Kate, more or less to herself.

"Oh, yes, it really could. And at least he isn't making a career of it, like recently deceased Jack Calloway." Louisa is heavily ironic.

Before she can stop herself, Kate asks, "Did you know about Jack and my mother?"

"My father and Jane Flickinger? Well, no, she's one I missed. But how on earth did you know?"

"She told me. You know Jane—she drinks a lot. She tells me a lot I'd just as soon not hear."

Louisa scowls. "Really, that's terrible—*terrible*. Of *course* Caroline would have known about that. It's frightening."

Watching her, Kate says, "Probably. But how do you mean—frightening?"

"His power, his devastation. You know—I think I told you—for a long time I thought I'd married Michael to get away from Jack—from his type, I mean. And then there was Bayard, exactly Jack's type. Although I never even met his wife—but I'm sure he let her know about me."

Understanding her (and thinking: I have met that goddam nurse), Kate says vaguely, "That's something, not meeting her."

Louisa continues intently, "It scares me about John—as though Jack might turn up in him somewhere. Somehow."

At that, Kate concentrates, and firmly says, "I don't think so." (But how about the other night. John and me? Suppose—suppose—And the idea is too terrible for her to finish.)

But then inexplicably Louisa laughs, and says, "Well, at least we like each other, John and I. That's one difference. I don't think Jack really liked anyone."

Kate laughs, too, in a sort of friendly agreement, and simultaneously they fall into the pool.

When they get out, they talk more easily. Kate says, "But it's not just sex that worries me with David, or an occasional nurse. He's begun to talk some funny other language—I don't mean about medicine; I'm used to that. Now it's so much about money—tax shelters, fiscal responsibility—whatever *they* are. Of course we've never really agreed about politics."

"John and I haven't even got there yet." Louisa manages to make this comic.

And so Kate laughs. "Well, he's probably not as Southern and conservative as he sounds." (She hopes this is true.)

So does Louisa.

"What I'd really like to do," Kate says, "is to get some sort of degree. Maybe psychiatric social work."

"As long as you don't end up sounding like Michael."

They laugh at this.

"I know it's corny," Kate rather shyly says, "but I like kids a lot. What used to be called adolescents. 'Hippies' now? Is that what Maude and Stephen are? Anyway, it must be my retarded development."

"But, Kate, you must do that; you'd be terrific—" Saying this, Louisa has an odd sense that she and Kate have shifted roles: it is unlike Kate to be shy, and ironically self-deprecating—unlike Louisa to be so positive. She is momentarily inhabiting Kate's mind, and in that moment she feels not only her friend's strength and generosity, but also some of Kate's pain. An amazing instant—but it goes, and she is only herself again, looking curiously and with sympathy at Kate.

And then it is time to go. They walk toward the house, past the old stables, the enormous formal boxwood, across the already yellowing lawn.

Eleven / 1968

At a table in the lobby of the Empress Hotel, in
Victoria, B.C., a man and a woman sit having their tea.
They are both extravagantly well dressed, but that is the sum
of their resemblance to each other. She is a huge (really
immense), florid, and formerly blond woman. She wears
prodigious jewelry, and the dark tweed jacket of her suit is
lined with mink. Her blue eyes look out from all that fat and
opulence with some surprise: this is not in any sense where
she would have expected to be. She, Grace Faulkner
(Magowan, Walters), fat and rich?

The man is in a gray suède suit that looks Italian; he is
very slender, dark and delicately featured. His eyes are
frightened (old permanent fears). And he is not as young as
he looks. Martin Walters (formerly Wasserman), who has
come a long way from his ugly mother's dinner table, from
Boston.

The other people having tea are a scattering of hotel
guests, rather nondescript, and some local regulars, who are
very British, old-style, in old tweeds and well-polished boots

and shoes, ruddy faces and dowdy graying hair. These people take Grace and Martin to be mother and son; this is a literal interpretation of what seems to be a difference in their ages, if physically unlikely. The more imaginative (and prurient) assume the connection to be somehow scandalous: they are so flauntingly rich.

Actually Martin is only a few years younger than Grace; closer inspection would show that his eyes are lined as well as shadowed. They have been married for ten days; while they travel, their new house in San Francisco is being "done."

"Or possibly they're married?"

"But he's a tearing pansy, from the look of him."

"Hubert, please! Do you think the scones are a little soggy?"

In her fortieth year far too many things happened to Grace: a daughter was institutionalized, perhaps for good. A rather distant New Hampshire relative died, and she inherited several million dollars that she had never known existed. She gained forty pounds. She met Martin. Grace was not equipped to cope with any of this—but who would be?

She had been such a shining perfect wife, all those bright hand-polished years. She saw the accumulated time of her marriage as a pile of loaves of bread, all the perfect bread she baked herself, a married woman brushing the bread with egg whites to perfect the crusts. And all the homemade clothes, the draperies and slipcovers. Three perfect children, until Allison refused to eat and vomited it all back at them—all the loaves and fish. Nothing was right after that; it was imperfect, flawed. Wrong. Sin is imperfection, and so she had to divorce Alex and to take Allison to New Hampshire, to go for long walks. To hide. But Allison got worse; she took sleeping pills, instead of apples from the hilly orchard. No good came to her from New Hampshire.

Her son Douglas wrote incomprehensible letters from a college in Oregon (Oregon?), all about wars. Wars and skiing. Snow. It made her numb.

Flicking his lashes, looking about, Martin says, "What an extraordinary place. Are you glad we came here? It rather reminds me of Boston."

"Darling, very glad." She munches at her cake.

"But I can't wait for you to see your house." He says this almost fiercely, fervently, his dark eyes intense upon her.

"Nor I." But houses are less important to her. Martin is important; she adores him.

All that money—thrifty Grace was shocked at the existence of so much, owned by one man; it was as though Uncle Justin had done something very dirty. She literally did not know what to do with it. Like someone in flight, she left New Hampshire and moved back to San Francisco, but of course the incorporeal money followed her. She moved into an old residential hotel in Pacific Heights—this was safe: Alex, now married to Sally, who was once Sally Chapin, had moved with her to Belvedere. (Sally was an almost perfect wife to Andrew Chapin, but not nearly so perfect as Grace. Sometimes Sally's bread would not rise, and she only waxed the floors twice a year.) Grace ate in the hotel's dining room—bland, really awful food—and she took to buying candies and little cakes from Fantasia and Blum's. She got very fat, and she got lonelier all the time.

Her suite of rooms, a penthouse, was large but drab, depressing. Listlessly Grace decided that she must do something. Buy things. God knows she could afford it: her unspent money kept piling up; larger figures added to larger ones, piling up like snow—as inevitable, as uncomforting.

She went for walks; she stared wistfully into windows, knowing that she could buy anything she wanted and finding nothing to buy.

Until one day, among a stretch of smart antique shops, along Sacramento Street, she saw in a window an ancient wooden doll, bald, in a tattered lace dress. She was seized with a violent and tearful nostalgia. She stood there staring, until from somewhere inside the shop a delicately handsome dark man appeared at her elbow—murmuring, "She's marvelous, isn't she?" (Later he is to say to Grace, "I've never thought of selling her, but she might be meant for you." Later still, the doll is a wedding present from Martin to Grace, his wife.)

Martin Walters. After his mother's death he quarreled (atrociously, and finally) with his father; he left Boston (and left his father's name). He came to San Francisco and set up shop as an antique dealer, a sometime decorator, for which he had a considerable flair. And he began to move in that curious (and nearly antiquated) social world in which homosexual men are used by rich "social" women as escorts (and they, of course, use the women as invitations—very possibly a fair exchange).

"I'm afraid I really don't know what I want," Grace told Martin, as they went into his store, that first day. "I live in a sort of hotel—it needs some decoration."

"Had you thought of getting a decorator?"

Of course she hadn't. But did he mean himself?

He did, and somewhat awkwardly they settled that he was to come for tea, and she named the hotel.

"Oh. Someone—a person I used to know lived there," said Martin.

She bought a lot of pastry, an orgy of small cakes, and some good Scotch, too, in case he would rather drink.

Martin arrived, and gave sensible advice. Concluding

(and reminding her) that she would not be there forever, he suggested a few small Oriental rugs, which could be taken anywhere, and a couple of good large lamps. Possibly new draperies.

That business out of the way, they began to talk. Grace said that she had recently come back from New Hampshire, and that led somehow back to her whole New England childhood (and his). Martin kept asking questions; he seemed fascinated by her childhood. Talking to Martin (and later when she was married to him), Grace felt that actually she was a little girl again, blond and frail and doted upon by relatives, instead of a grown-up woman (forty!) accidentally encased in fat.

They talked for hours. It seemed natural for Grace to skim over the recent unhappy events of her life, and to dwell on the golden autumn leaves of New England Octobers, the bluish moonlit fields of snow.

Later Martin took her out to dinner, to a small French restaurant in the avenues, where they drank a lot of wine and went on talking.

When they got back to her hotel, he kissed her very gently on the cheek. "After you're grown up, it's not very often you make a new friend," he said.

Grace went up to her room and cried herself to sleep, as she hadn't since she was a child.

They began to see each other a great deal.

At first Grace thought, Well, of course he's homosexual; and then she thought, Well, perhaps not. And then she more or less stopped thinking along those lines.

Martin told her that for a long time he had been very much afraid of women. "Except for a wonderful friend named Barbara Spaulding. You must meet her, and Eliot, her husband. From Boston."

Sometimes, in a way that seemed to Grace both mild and sweet, they kissed, and (mildly) caressed each other.

Martin's favorite line, often quoted to Grace, was from Bob Dylan: "If you're not busy changing, you're busy dying."

Grace at last began to understand that she was madly, totally in love with this man. She wanted to make love to him—yes, that is exactly what she wanted to do. She had what were to her shocking fantasies about his dark thin body. Things that she had never done with Alex.

But it is Martin who finally suggests, as they sit there kissing and caressing (mildly still): "We could get in bed and take off our clothes, you know—under the covers?"

With their backs to each other, standing apart, they do undress. They turn off lights; they meet under layers of blankets in Grace's not very wide bed. Her hands seek him out—he is soft. Grace finds this reassuring, as his gentleness has always reassured her. He whispers to her, "I'm very slow, are you? I thought you would be."

And so they lie there, slowly touching each other, meeting gently in a kiss.

Grace finds this beautiful. His body is incredibly beautiful.

They decide to marry. Grace is radiant.

To Alex the whole thing is very embarrassing. "I never really would have thought—" he says to Sally; he is flushed, and serious veins throb in his forehead. "I mean, can't she see—or didn't anyone *say* to her—"

"I'm not sure," Sally says softly. "You know I haven't seen her for years."

"But doesn't she *know*—I hate to see poor Grace exploited like this," he at last bursts out. "By some—some *queer*, in fact a Jewish queer. Christ, he's even changed his name."

Andrew Chapin and Isabel, his wife, have somewhat more literary conversations about the same thing. "Of course, the point of interest, as I see it," Andrew says, "would be Grace's attitude toward his history."

"Maybe she pretends it isn't there?" Isabel is very bright, and Andrew has increased her confidence.

He is impressed. "You're very intuitive," he says, not for the first time. "How like Grace that would be. Just the way she used to pretend that Allison wasn't crazy."

Encouraged, Isabel goes on. "And of course if Grace is successful in her pretending she will help him erase that past. He can breathe easily, so to speak."

"Exactly."

This conversation takes place at breakfast. Pretty young Isabel is still in her rumpled yellow robe, her face shiny, unmade-up; her habits are fortunately quite unlike those of the former Sally Chapin. Now Andrew reaches around to kiss her soft mouth. These two people like each other very much.

Martin Walters and his brother Michael Wasserman have an odd relationship—odd in that they almost never see each other; what contact they have takes place over the phone. And it is almost always Michael who phones, who has felt some lonely lack—a need for his brother. Michael in fact would like to talk about their family, to recreate and endlessly interpret those dynamics: "What do you suppose their sex life was really like? She must have been frigid, don't you think? You know, really Louisa was more of a *father* figure for me—" But Martin (understandably enough) will have less and less of this. And Persephone comforts Michael: "He's transferred his ambivalence about his father onto you."

After Martin's marriage the two brothers talk even less; for one thing (perhaps unconsciously), they would both want to avoid the broad humor implicit in the fact of fat rich wives for both of them. (What does this mean?) And, curiously, Michael is at his meanest when speaking of Grace. "Good old Grace," he says. "I always knew those big cans of hers were misleading. She could be in drag herself."

Fat Persephone, who adores him, laughs at this.

"Of course the real point," Michael tells her, "is whether or not he can get it up with women."

This is another "good marriage." (Is there someone for everyone?)

From Victoria, Grace and Martin take the boat down to Seattle, among the beautiful dark wooded islands, the San Juan straits. In Seattle they are to separate for twenty-four hours. This is Martin's idea, which Grace does not like. But he wants to see to the installation of all the things in their new Green Street house before she does. He insists. "It has to be perfect before you see it, love."

"But suppose something's wrong, something you have to fix: am I supposed to spend a week in Seattle?"

He laughs lightly, and with great affection. "No, my darling. We'll meet and fly to Mexico for a week, in that case."

Reassured, she wanders around Seattle for a day, buying presents for everyone: her daughters, Allison and Jennifer, mainly for Martin. (In her happiness she has almost forgotten where Allison is.)

Of course they telephone to each other that night. Martin's voice is excited; she could almost believe him drunk, except that she knows he hardly drinks at all.

He has what strikes Grace as a rather curious plan. "This may seem very unchivalrous," he says—sounding Southern, which at times he does. "But would you take a cab from the airport to Green Street? Just come right here?"

"You won't meet me?" She is disappointed, even hurt.

"Darling, love—I want to watch you walk into your house."

She does; she walks into her house. She sees shining chrome, gray suède and polished oak, patterned velvet, heavy wicker, heavy wool carpeting. Paintings, bronzes. Flowers—spring flowers in bowls placed everywhere. She sees Martin—she runs to him and hides her face against his tweed. She cries, she repeats and repeats his name.

It is a marriage that continues to be discussed. A year later there are still snickers among some of Martin's former friends. (Actually he had quite a lot of friends—or semi-friends, if true friends are only those who wish one well.) They giggle about Grace's weight; they predict young boys within a year for Martin. (Inaccurately: he remains almost religiously faithful to Grace.)

Martin and Grace see even less of Michael and Persephone—which, except for lingering in vestigial guilts, is fine with everyone.

After one meeting (a characteristic failure: a smart

French restaurant to which Michael has refused to wear a tie, and only Martin's "pull" gets them in) Persephone complains, "He makes her so childish—he encourages Grace to be a little girl." (Which is perhaps what Persephone would like, in part, to be, and which is not at all the role that Michael assigns to her.)

Michael answers, "Of course he wants her to be a child; what on earth would Martin do with a grown-up woman?"

(It is not fair to say, as Louisa sometimes does, that Michael is totally imperceptive.)

Alex Magowan remains outraged. Just below the surface of his mind is a sense of Martin as a threat to his own manhood, his own virility: how could Grace, who was married to him, go on to *that?*

His youngest daughter, Jennifer, tries to explain. Over and against his mutterings she says, "Father, you're entirely missing the point. Martin is extremely nice to Mother. He made that fabulous house for her, he keeps it filled with flowers, he brings her presents—"

"But with her money—it's all her money!"

"So what? What does it matter whose money it is? The point is," Jennifer repeats, "the point is that mother is very happy. She's never been happier in her life."

And Jennifer is absolutely right: Grace has never been so happy in her life.

Twelve / 1969

The grounds are beautifully kept; people always notice and mention the grounds, as though they had expected something else. Green lawns, even and stretching out to distances, trimmed green shrubbery and tidy trees. Eucalyptuses would make a mess, and besides in a wind they are noisy.

Allison is waiting. A list of people are coming to see her this afternoon. Her father, called Father, and Alex, who is her mother's former husband. Her mother speaks sadly of "Alex." And Mrs. Chapin and Sally and her father's wife, Mrs. Alexander Magowan.

"How many does that make?" Allison asks her friend Mary, who is waiting on the bench with her.

"Two. Three at most," says Mary.

Mary is extremely fat, and Allison wishes that she would go away. It is too hot to be with such a heavy friend. And she herself is so excruciatingly thin. She is aware that they look silly together. They sit on the white concrete bench where Allison has said that she would meet her people, two contrasting girls in the overwhelming September noon, in Napa, California.

Where are all the people who are coming? Allison looks at all the slowly passing cars, who are looking at her, but there are no cars with groups. People seem to come in twos. Mary has gone, perhaps melted. It is hot enough.

Two people are coming toward Allison on the sidewalk. An angry man, and a woman at his heels. At his heels? Both people are tanned, darkly tanned, as though from vacations, or boats; they both have sun-bleached hair. Possibly they are related. Allison knows the man, although she has forgotten his name.

"Allison! What are you doing here? I told you we'd meet you at the—uh—dormitory. We've been waiting there for half an hour."

Or perhaps she doesn't know him.

"Darling, it's all right, we've found her," the woman says in an exceptionally soft voice. "Allison, dear, how are you?" She comes very close to Allison, smelling sweet, a little too sweet.

Loudly her father, whose name is Alexander Magowan, says, "You remember Sally?"

"Mrs. Chapin?"

"Yes, of course she used to be Mrs. Chapin, but you remember, we got married two years ago, and now she's Mrs. Magowan—Sally."

"Sally," says Mrs. Chapin-Magowan softly.

Mary is right, and all those people—those visitors —are only two. The truth often turns out to be so simple, simple and boring and ultimately to be resisted.

"Well," says Father, "how about coming out to lunch with us? I got your—uh—pass." He hates it that Allison is here.

"My, what lovely grounds," says Mrs. Chapin-Sally.

In New Hampshire, where Allison lived with her mother, the birch trees littered the grass with leaves and peelings.

They are walking toward her father's car. "Oh, a new car," says Allison.

No longer angry—in fact very pleased and surprised that she has noticed—Father says, "Yes, you like it? I really don't think you can beat the Germans when it comes to making cars."

Beat the Germans?

Allison gets into the back seat, her own wide space of dark new leather. Far apart in the front seat are her father and Sally Chapin, who has three children, boys. Allison has a brother, Douglas, who is up at school in Oregon, Reed College. He writes her letters. He is crazy. People believe that he is interested in history; it is clear to Allison that he only likes wars. His madness is her private treasure.

"Where would you like to go for lunch? Do you know a place?"

"Oh, anywhere. I still don't eat very much."

Father clears his throat. "Your—uh—mother was here last week?"

Allison concentrates. "I think so." Her mother's name is Grace. Mary, who was once a Catholic, thinks that is very funny. "Mary full of Grace," says Mary. "I am full of your mother. That's enough to make anyone fat. Perhaps I am your mother."

Smiling at the thought of Mary, Allison says, "Grace."

"That's right," says Sally softly. "Grace. Grace and Martin. Grace is married to Martin. Did he come up with her?"

"There seems to be a lot of marrying going on," says Allison, more loudly than she meant to. But there are too many names. She decides that there should not be names; names are boundaries separating people, preventing a confluence from one into another.

Then still another name comes into her mind, and she asks, "Who is Andrew?"

Sally's face pinkens. "Andrew used to be my husband, when you knew us both a long time ago. Then we were divorced, and I married your father, Alex." Why does she speak so softly? Is she ashamed of what she is saying?

They cross a river on a narrow bridge. The water is thickly lined with leaning trees, willows and whispering eucalyptuses. Free boys stand beside the water with fishing poles, but they will never catch anything.

In New Hampshire, Allison and her mother, Grace, went endlessly for walks, endlessly up and down those hard white roads, past sweet meadows with stone fences, past dark secret woods. Grace thought enough walking would cure anything, but she was wrong. It didn't even develop an appetite in Allison. So that now she is here.

Her brother Douglas writes mad letters to his sister Allison. "All the scruffy longhairs around here hope we'll be out of the fighting soon," he writes. "Not me. I'm heading for the Marine Corps. I want to be permanently a Marine." Douglas has been studying the forties, that war; he believes that now is then. It is clear to Allison that he is quite mad; in fact she carries the madness of Douglas within her. She is pregnant with her brother's madness, although it doesn't show.

Her father, Alex, and his wife, Sally Chapin, have come to tell her something, perhaps about Douglas. They are burdened with a heavy message to give her. Their faces sag with some oppressive knowledge.

"—eat here?" They have stopped at a shopping center, in front of a restaurant that says "SMORGAS-

BORD." They won't like it inside because there are no drinks. Allison was here with some other people last week. Grace and someone. Mary full of Grace?

"Okay," says Allison.

They go inside and sit down.

"You have to get up and get a tray and walk around with it," Allison tells them.

"Oh?" They are very interested. "You were here before?"

Dishonestly she points to a sign. "Over there. It says."

"Oh." Disappointed.

They do what the sign says. (What Grace said —Grace and Martin?) They put indistinguishable things onto their plates.

Father asks, "How's the food at the—uh—hospital?"

"It's really lousy."

"Darling, for a minute she sounded exactly like you!" Mrs. Chapin sounds like herself, soft and very surprised.

But what is remarkable about that? They are all the same person: how should they sound?

Today, even more than usual, Douglas keeps flashing into Allison's mind. Douglas everywhere, all ages and sizes of Douglas. Small Douglas, on top of a fence.

"No drinks, I guess," says Alex, her father. His red-tan face darkens.

"Darling, it's possibly just as well?" Sweet Sally.

"Did Douglas jump off the fence that time, or fall?" asks Allison.

"He jumped," says Alex, his face suddenly full of some terrible pain.

"Not now," Sally murmurs, and she touches his hand.

At the other tables are other people whom Allison has

seen before. Perhaps some of them are also patients who are out for lunch with their visitors? Alex and Sally wonder this, too, but they are too polite to ask.

Since they have one definite thing to say to her, but have decided to postpone its saying, it is hard for Alex and Sally Chapin-Magowan to talk to Allison. She would like to help them out but she is not sure how.

"I have a friend named Mary," she tells them.

"Oh, really. Isn't that nice."

But there again they are stopped. They can't think of a further thing to ask about Mary, because what they really would like to know about Mary is what's wrong with her; why is she here?

Allison tries to tell them. "I guess we both sort of fit into the landscape there," she says. They don't know what she means, but they are afraid to say so. "Mary is extremely fat," she explains. Then she thinks of "full of Grace," and she begins to laugh.

They smile sadly at her, thinking, She is not getting any better.

In fact, the time that Douglas jumped, they were all there: Sally and Andrew Chapin and their three boys; and Alex Magowan and Grace, his wife, and their three children, Douglas and Allison and Jennifer. Jennifer?

"Jennifer?" Allison asks.

"Oh, Jennifer's just fine. She's finishing up at Miss Hamlin's and then she's thinking about Stanford."

"I don't remember her terribly well," says Allison, wanting to be honest.

"Your sister?" They try to believe what she has said.

"I remember Douglas all the time."

Her father pours milk into his coffee. "Douglas—had an accident," he says.

What they are going to tell her will not necessarily be true.

"He was skiing," says Alex slowly.

"What is 'skiing'?" Allison asks politely.

"What is *skiing?* Allison, Squaw *Valley*—we went there every year." He turns to Sally, to his wife. "I know it's beside the point, but do you have any idea what it costs these days to take three kids skiing for a week?" Back to Allison, he wildly continues. "Skiing—snow, going down mountains. You do remember?"

She remembers something: cold, being afraid. But she has to resist. "Not really," she says, very softly. (Is she turning into Sally, Mrs. Chapin; into her father's wife?)

Her father and Sally Chapin look at each other. "Maybe not now," says Mrs. Chapin. "After all, we've waited this long—"

Relief rises in Allison's throat, but it has the taste of bile.

And there is still the problem of conversation. "I have a friend named Mary," Allison says before she remembers having already said that. "She's been there much longer than I have." She did not tell them that before; she is sure of it.

They try to look interested. "Much longer?"

"Three months longer." This could quite possibly be true, but it was the wrong thing to say: how can she be sure of a number when she doesn't know what skiing is? "Of course I could be wrong," she adds, and then this strikes her as very funny, and she laughs "inappropriately."

"Well, shall we go? Everyone had enough?"

Their pushed chairs make a very loud noise on the restaurant floor. Three chairs.

"Is this a new car?" asks Allison, but this time they are not pleased at her question—of course not.

"Yes." Her father frowns, with no mention of beating Germans.

They all get into the car. They take off.

Alex and Sally. Grace and Martin. Musingly Allison says these name combinations over to herself. Allison and Douglas. Who?

They again pass the river, the messy eucalyptus trees. The boys fishing there.

Her father, who has given up telling Allison anything, now would like to ask her something. He clears his throat. "Do they say anything to you about—uh—getting out?"

His question for an instant terrifies Allison. Out? In her new soft voice, she asks him, "Where is out?"

They give up.

They begin to talk between themselves, as though Allison were not there, or as they might have done if she only spoke and understood some foreign language. Korean. Vietnamese.

"There seemed no point—"

"No, why add—"

"I suppose I should talk—"

"I suppose."

They return to the beginning of the beautifully kept grounds.

Feeling better and wanting to help them—her helpless visitors stranded there in the front seat—Allison with an effort presents a memory, a gift. "Once at Squaw Valley Douglas told me that if you skied out over the headwall, at Siberia, you would fly, fly for the rest of your life. I thought he was kidding but he wasn't, and he was angry that I wouldn't try it. But Douglas is very handsome, isn't he? The best-looking one of us."

She has not helped at all. Parting from her, their faces are anguished, so that Allison is seized with a wrenching, helpless pity for them both—for them all, whoever they are.

· · ·

They go away and Allison finds Mary. "It was okay," she says, "but where we went for lunch was really lousy, although everyone seems to go there."

"Yes," says her friend.

"I think they wanted to tell me something about Douglas, but I saw absolutely no point in letting them do that. Why add?"

"Yes."

Thirteen / 1970 (1971)

In an enormous raftered house on outer Broadway in San Francisco, Louisa and John Jeffreys are celebrating the early hours of New Year's Eve with the people who live in that house, with Maude and some of her friends.

The house, a Victorian mansion, has been scheduled for destruction. It was bought by an extremely successful Italian builder, who is a distant cousin of the mayor's. Here, in an elegant neighborhood, on a block with a stupendous view of the Bay and Marin County, the builder will put yet another high-rise, apartments for which he can charge exalted rents. The kids are allowed to rent the house from month to month, for what comes to around fifty dollars a month apiece; there are quite a few of them. (It is not, strictly speaking, a commune—just friends living in the same house.) This arrangement came about because one of the kids is the son of a lawyer who is close to the mayor, and who is also a friend of the builder's. It makes everyone, including the mayor, feel pleasantly tolerant; they are being nice to hippies.

The young people do not seem to be made nervous by the imminent destruction of their house. They feel that by then they may want to move on, anyway. Also they do not think in terms of a distant future (reasonably enough, for their generation).

The great rooms with distant dusky ceilings and narrow mullioned windows are somewhat overwhelming, resistant to change. But the kids have done their best. A shawl draped here, another there—posters, driftwood sculpture. And for their party they have made a great effort at tidying up.

So many young people. Thirty or so. It is not at all clear to Louisa and John which of them live there, which ones are guests for the evening. It is even less clear what the relationships within the group might be.

A few of them are recognized as old friends. Jennifer Magowan is there, and Allison—skinny frightened Allison, out from Napa on a pass; she sits in a corner drinking wine, pouring wine down her throat—she can't last long. Jennifer is with Stephen Harrington, the son of Kate, Louisa's friend. Stephen has Kate's dark red hair, which he wears very long, and her long sexy eyes. And a full beard.

And others, unknown—some introduced, some not:

A small blond girl in a long dress that must be her idea of a forties costume: calf-length, sequined. Thirties? It is not really a look that Louisa or John can remember. But the girl reminds Louisa dimly of someone from a long time ago; she seems vaguely Southern, and finally it comes to her. She nudges John. "Do you remember Snubby MacDonald?" "No—" "John, you were in love with her, before Kate!" "Well, sort of. Blond?" "You don't even remember! I remember everything that ever happened." (She does.)

Two girls in bright red loosely crocheted dresses,

clearly made by one of them; they both have black curly hair and big noses. Sisters.

A tall somewhat frail-looking boy named Jonathan. (Louisa stares at him, not knowing why, and then she understands that he looks a little like Maude—a boy Maude.)

A dark sturdy bearded boy.

(Few of them have names; none have last names.)

Louisa and John have spent Christmas in Mexico —Oaxaca—they are both splendidly tanned: John with his very white hair, Louisa with her dark hair fashionably streaked blond. They have not seen Maude for a month or so. And they see that something extraordinary has happened in that month: Maude has turned beautiful. From being a pale, somewhat sickly, too tall and too thin girl, she has become a beautiful young woman. Still tall and thin, still delicate, her frailness now is controlled—is lovely. Her skin shines. Her long face is witty and intelligent—is happy. Even (incongruous on her thin body) her full loose breasts look proud. Feeling that the unattractive old phrase "flatchested" was made especially for herself, Louisa sees an irony in this; and then it comes to her that, of course, Maude's breasts are a gift from her grandmother, horrible fat Mrs. Wasserman.

Looking at her lovely daughter, Louisa is amazed; she would not dare to take credit for Maude. And she wonders: Is Maude now beautiful for good, or is this simply a moment in her life?

Although of course they were invited, Louisa and John are actually spectators at the party. They stand together, apart from the rest, in a tentative position near the door. They talk to each other. They are glad to be there, they smile in an appreciative way, but they do not have a lot to say to most of "the children."

The connection between Jennifer and Kate's boy Stephen is at least superficially clear: they are lovers, they live together. Jennifer looks at him in an amused, protective way; his look at her is mildly irritated and very sexual. His sexy look reminds Louisa strongly of his mother—of sexy young Kate, years back, on the dance floor of the decorated high school gymnasium (the Tin Can). Louisa remembers how John looked at Kate, back then, and now she looks jealously at him, as though all that had just happened. She is still powerfully attracted to John, and she thinks that later —in fact soon—they will go home and smoke grass, and make love.

So far, this evening, there are no drugs in evidence in the room. For various reasons this particular group of kids uses very little drugs.

Maude has come over to where Louisa and John are standing. Close up she is even prettier. She is wearing a long gauzy flowered dress, all shades of pink, that is very becoming to her own delicacy. And that is what her mother chooses to say. "What a pretty dress. It's really perfect for you."

"Thanks. I like it a lot. Jennifer made it for me, for Christmas."

"Really? She made it? But that's terrific."

But then, as often with Maude or with others of her age, Louisa has begun to feel that she overdoes what she is saying, that her style is over emphatic. They say so little, these children. They so steadfastly refuse effusion.

And Maude's voice is so soft and delicate, so gentle. She visibly and audibly tries to be nice to her mother. "You look great, too," she says. "Are you going on to another party?"

Does this mean are you leaving soon? Louisa imagines this (of course) and then reminds herself that Maude is never so crude.

Soon afterward John and Louisa do leave, and they begin the long drive toward the hills of Berkeley, where they have recently bought a house.

At times (as even "happily married" women will) Louisa has a lonely sense that she and John don't *talk*. How she yearns for more conversation, for in fact the sort of conversation that she often has with Kate. Can one have personal conversations only with women? And she thinks then of a succession of men who wouldn't talk with her (Michael talked *at*). Instead of talking (perhaps) she works, alone, and she and John make love.

In other moods she romanticizes their relationship, and she tells herself that their lengthy frame of reference makes talk unnecessary—simply to be together is to communicate.

(Perhaps both are true?)

However, tonight they are talking—a lot.

"You know one thing that's marvelous?" Louisa now says. "Those fat girls in the awful crocheted dresses. In our day they'd have been hiding in corners. 'Wallflowers.' But they looked perfectly pleased with themselves."

"Did they? I didn't notice."

"Darling, they were right there." She laughs. "They'd never have made it into the Sub-Deb Club."

"That blonde was sort of dreadful."

"I thought she was real cute."

"You're teasing."

"Yes, I am."

"Odd that she was with such a faggy boy."

"Which boy?"

"Poor Allison doesn't look much better. God, she's so thin."

"I never saw her before, did I?"

"No, but she doesn't. When I remember her parents, Grace and Alex, all those years ago—of all people to have a crazy child. And there was something about her brother going over a headwall on purpose."

"The terrible familiar stories."

"Yes."

They have reached the Bay Bridge. Lights. Streaming cars above the black water. Not the bridge for suicides, but grim enough, at night, on the lower ramp. The night is unseasonably clear for California; this is usually a season of lashing dark rains, enveloping a persecuted city. Tonight is not only clear but freakishly warm, almost a Southern night—both Louisa and John think but do not say this; they shy off what might be sentimental. But the strange weather has excited them, has created in both of them a certain heightened mood.

Of the weather Louisa only remarks, "There's going to be one of those extraordinary false springs. I can tell. With that bright unreal grass breaking out everywhere. Under the trees in parks."

"Did that happen last year?"

"Yes, but later on, I think."

They laugh, although nothing is expecially funny. They laugh as though already high.

"How beautiful Maude is," Louisa says at last; it is what she has been wanting to say all along.

"Yes, very." John says this seriously—he knows how seriously Louisa takes her daughter.

"When I think how I used to worry, God! I thought she had to be some sort of cripple."

"You mean, like you?"

She understands him, and she is filled with pleasure. Which she must deny. "Well, I used to be sort of crippled," she says.

"Sort of crippled—that suggests an interesting way of walking, I must say."

They laugh again, very affectionate with each other.

They have passed the U.C. campus, and begun the winding climb into the hills, the narrow eucalyptus-lined streets, that smell of lemon.

"But which boy was Maude *with?*" Louisa asks, as though John would know.

He laughs at her. "Darling, you're so conventional. Does she have to be with anyone?"

She frowns, never good at being teased. "You know what I mean."

"You mean, which one is she screwing." (This is not a word that John ordinarily uses; does he mean to suggest disapproval? This is possible.) "Maybe all of them, maybe everyone in the room. Girls, too."

"You and your dirty-old-man fantasies."

But she is right; he is a little turned on by what he is saying. He goes on, "Maybe right now, since we're gone, they're all having an orgy with each other."

For several reasons, some of which she does not recognize, Louisa does not like this at all. Partly, she is jealous: much easier to imagine John at an orgy than herself, John with a lot of young girls. (With Maude?) She does not stop herself from saying, "In that case perhaps you should go back?"

He hears what is in her voice, and says, "I'd much rather go home with you." He is a nice man, as well as being Southern.

Louisa feels a melting within herself, and a disbelief: he does then love her?

The house that Louisa and John have finally bought is an older house (fifty years, which is old for California), Spanish style, with long arched windows that overlook the Bay, a red mansard roof. They spent a year or so looking at lots and talking to architects, until it came to both of them, simultaneously, that they didn't want to build a house; they wanted one that was already there, settled into the land. They spent more time looking at houses. Maybecks and imitation Maybecks, until on an October afternoon they saw this one, surrounded by bright Japanese maples, and they recognized it as their own.

Now they go inside and settle on the broad gray velvet sofa, Louisa in her long white wool dress (it is always hard for her to decide what to wear, visiting "the children"; she chose an old favorite), John in his habitual gray flannels and tweed.

Lights have been left on in their dining room and kitchen; here they turn nothing on. Through the long Moorish windows they can see the lights all over the hills of

San Francisco, the lights of both bridges, and the few stray lights from boats about the Bay. A view so glamorous that they are still not used to it, as neither of them is really used to California (but who could live in the South, they say to each other), even though Louisa has been in California for what is now most of her life.

The house could be read as an expression of Louisa's (and John's) attitude toward money and "things," which could be summarized as: Well, we have it, why not? Nothing ostentatious, but everything very "good." Good Oriental rugs and linen draperies, brown quilted leather on matching armchairs. The huge gray velvet sofa.

And very good pictures: a small (real) Klee, two Picasso drawings, a Matisse. A large painting by James Boynton, over the mantel.

Perhaps curiously, there is nothing of Louisa's on display, although by now she has had several shows, is represented in several galleries. "I'd be embarrassed" is her disappointing explanation.

There are some large framed photographs by John. (He has, in San Francisco, taken up photography. He is very good.) Victorian houses. Whales spouting, out at sea—from the Mendocino coast. Louisa, in her studio (his best).

New Year's Eve, in common with other major holidays, enforces memories of other New Years. Louisa remembers a dismal psychologists' party, with Michael, and then a desperate night with (or, rather, without) Bayard. And, before either of those, a terrible party at home, in Hilton, with the Flickingers (Kate's parents). Jack contemptuously courting Jane Flickinger. Kate off somewhere else (with John?). Jack drunk and mean, Caroline weeping in her room. Determinedly shaking all that off (and at the same time wondering what John remembers; she is still jealous of his past), Louisa says, "What a perfect way to spend New Year's Eve, isn't it?" She has been struck by the sentimental thought that John is her defense against her past; she feels the bravado of a second marriage.

(But why will he never speak to her of his first marriage? Is she—Louisa—not also his friend? She thinks sometimes that Southern John would consider any reference to a dead—a suicided—wife as tasteless, but the fact of his not mentioning Lois keeps her very present to Louisa. And the similarity of names—how ominous! Louisa thinks frequently of Lois, and wonders everything about her. How beautiful was she? What did she like to do in bed? Was she bright, as well? All impossible, unimaginable questions, in terms of John. And she is reminded, of course, of King—of the presence of "Bobbie" in their "affair." Does she somehow need Lois?)

She asks, "Shall I get the champagne?"

"I'll get it." Lightly, he has already stood up. "Are the joints on your dresser?"

"Yes."

He goes out, and comes back with the wine, chilled glasses, ashtray and matches, and two neat thick joints—all ceremoniously on a silver tray. He opens the bottle deftly, a napkin held over the cork. He pours.

They touch glasses. Smile, take sips. Lean toward each other in a light warm kiss. They put down the glasses to light the joints.

"Wow, it really tastes good."

Smoking grass, they tend to sound like kids. But it is an important addition to their life. They much prefer it to booze; in fact they drink a lot less, wanting to savor the high.

Somewhat later one of them says, "I don't feel a thing, do you?"

An old joke between them, at which they both laugh.

They turn to each other, and for what seems like several hours, but is actually more like numbered minutes, they make love.

What is happening back at the house where the children live is not an orgy but an argument. What to do next: they are all (all but Allison) in various ways involved in this. Their party was planned as an early evening event, an interim before more important plans—in some cases, before obligations to parents and parents' parties. The (faggy) son of the well-connected lawyer, however, has no such obligations, or if he does, "Well, screw them," he unconvincingly says. He wants to go to see the Cockettes, the midnight transvestite show at the Palace Theatre, and he wants the burly son of the cop to come with him.

"Oh, come on, it'll broaden you."

As titillated as he is frightened, the boy tries to be gruff. "It sounds ridiculous. Why not just go to Finnocchio's with the rest of the tourists and be done with it?"

"Oh, but they're so old."

A nervous laugh. "Suppose the Cockettes get busted and it's my old man who makes the bust?"

"Well I think that would be a real gas. Then my old man could get us off. But we won't be all that lucky."

A girl squeals, "Can I come, too? Oh, the Cockettes, how *neat!*"

Another group departs for a midnight show of *2001*, along with several old Beatles movies: classics from their early adolescence.

The fat red crocheted girls are with that nostalgic group.

Allison has passed out on a small Victorian horsehair sofa—from a combination of fear and fatigue and too much wine.

Maude argues (who should stay with Allison) on the basis of numbers. "You see? Between you and Stephen, you have three parties. You'd be disappointing three groups. For me there's just Dad and Persephone. They'll talk about it a lot but I don't think they'll really care."

Jennifer knows that all her people will care, and that she will worry about their caring. She says, "Okay, you're really nice to take care of her. Poor old Allison." Worriedly she smiles down at her sister.

Stephen says, "Oh, Jennifer, come on. We'll never get to all those places that you say we have to get to."

She smooths her hand over his high hard buttocks. "Oh, Steve, calm down."

They leave.

"Listen, Dad, Allison's had too much wine, so I said I'd stay and take care of her."

"But can you?" (Persephone is also on the line; they have answered the phone simultaneously, as they often do.) "Let's see, Ian McMillan is coming soon, and I could *easily*—" Persephone always knows a lot of doctors; next to food, medicine is what she most likes to talk about.

From the other phone Michael addresses himself to Persephone. "Now, honey, don't you worry about Allison. Maude is perfectly capable—"

"But Allison's been so sick. It might be some sort of catatonia. I mean I don't see how Maude—"

"If anything goes wrong, Maude will call us, won't—"

"But I made all those little anise cookies, I thought Maude—"

They are both enjoying this exchange, but Maude breaks into it. She says, "I'm really okay. I'll just watch her. Have a good party."

"Darling, yes! Happy New Year!"

"Happy—"

"Good night—"

As Maude hangs up, Jonathan comes into the room.

"Oh, hi. I forgot you were here."

"Thanks a lot."

But they grin at each other. Good friends. In fact they do look alike. Tall thin fair people, somewhat delicate. Long noses, large eyes. Jonathan is wearing Levis, a clean unironed blue work shirt.

"She looks uncomfortable." Jonathan goes over to where Allison is (indeed) uncomfortably sprawled on the too small sofa. Gently he lifts her legs up and stretches them out, over the arm of the sofa.

Allison sighs in her sleep, then wakes and looks at him. She is frightened. "Douglas?"

"No, Jonathan. And Maude."

"Oh." She smiles, and goes back to sleep.

Stephen and Jennifer go first to her mother's house. Grace and Martin. ("Let's get them over with first.") Jennifer does not dislike her mother; she is genuinely glad that Grace is happy with Martin, but she has less and less to say to them.

It is actually a reception, rather than a party, that Grace and Martin are having. A reception honoring the new year, and themselves. Their sparkling house still looks brand-new. Possessions have been added, and they have a lot of shining new friends: rich successful glossy people —somewhat like themselves, somewhat unreal. Women in long opulent dresses, graying men in black ties. Waiters in white gloves.

Barbara and Eliot Spaulding, who still think of themselves as Bostonians. (By now, when Barbara makes her remark about the first Jews she ever met being horrible, she forgets that Martin was one of them—and so does he.)

People are saying things like:

"You don't see much of this sort of thing any more."

"No, people just don't."

"Well, Grace and Martin really know."

"All the stops."

What Stephen says to Jennifer is "Jesus Christ. Don't these people know there's a war on?"

Although he is of course serious, she (of course) laughs, and they head toward her mother—majestic Grace, in cream-colored satin and diamonds. (Martin chooses her clothes and buys her jewelry.)

At the sight of her daughter, Grace frowns a little, as though she were not entirely sure who Jennifer is. And in a sense she is not; often weeks pass in which she does not think of her youngest child, and she has successfully put Allison out of her mind. And Douglas—she never thinks of Douglas. What she does feel about Jennifer is that she can take care of herself, and in that she is fortunately correct.

(But that taking care requires more of an effort from Jennifer than almost anyone is aware of; even Stephen tends to take her steady pleasant competence for granted.)

With an effort Jennifer tells her mother that she looks marvelous, that it is a marvelous party; she is sorry they have to leave so soon.

Stephen makes no conciliatory effort at all. Visibly out of place, with his beard and long red hair (World War II Army surplus clothes), his stance and expression make it clear that he is there by accident; it is not his scene at all.

"Do let me get you some champagne," says elegant Martin, who believes his outrage to be well concealed. ("God, Grace, darling, *why* do they have to come?")

"No, thanks, we're on our way out."

"You don't find all that hair a nuisance to take care of?" (This is envious; Martin's own hair has begun to thin.)

"No." Stephen gives him a level, long-eyed look.

Unreasonably frightened (Stephen is a kindly boy), Martin retreats (as he has before) into girlishness, a girl that no one could possibly hurt. He simpers, "Well, I didn't mean—" and he walks away, mincing more than he has for years.

Grace and Martin are happiest alone; dangers lurk in any social life for them. Later in the evening they will wonder why on earth they had to give a party. Next year they won't.

In contrast to Grace, her former husband, Alex Magowan, talks of Allison obsessively, and especially to Jennifer. (Which is another burden that she bears well.)

And, further contrast, the party that Alex and Sally give is informal, unpretentious almost to the point of being a pretense in itself. They live in a huge (expensive) house —rustic, raftered—in Belvedere, on the water. A house that Alex designed. All the rooms are open to each other, and open to the Bay—no secrets in that house. (No privacy.) They live there with Sally's three boys, and three very large Irish setters, all beautiful and hysterical and not very bright, and a mean destructive collection of Siamese cats, who have shredded most of the furniture and smelled up several rooms.

Sally has made an interesting (so far only half-admitted) discovery about herself, which is that she very much dislikes most people. (Could that explain her soft voice? If she spoke out, she might say something angry?) She is not really fond of animals, either. (Hence the behavior of the cats, who are very intelligent.) She especially dislikes guests; always an indifferent hostess, she has got worse.

"Oh, but you're so *dressed up*" is her greeting to Jennifer, spoken as softly as ever. "Stephen, dear, how nice to see you." She looks about her, and gives a little laugh. "I just can't imagine why we're giving a New Year's Eve party."

The blond down on Sally's chin has become bristly; sometimes it occurs to her to "have something done about it"; at other times she thinks: Oh, why? And she takes a tiny pleasure in what she (to herself) refers to as "my beard." She suspects (correctly) that Alex likes it. Andrew always did.

Alex frowns at Jennifer. "You didn't bring Allison?"

Jennifer sighs. There is really no point in telling him anything. They have talked so much about Allison, and he will never believe that she is crazy. She says, "No, she was really tired. She went to sleep."

"To sleep? This early? Where?" Alex is eager to externalize blame for Allison; it is obvious to him that evil outside forces put Allison to sleep.

"At Maude's. You know, the house out on Broadway where Maude Wasserman and some other kids live."

"Oh, yes." (Poor Alex still finds the cluster of second marriages awkward, as well as in poor taste.)

There are a lot of guests that night at the Magowans'. Suburban couples in imported turtleneck sweaters and stained Levis. ("Sally *said* not to dress.") They sit about on the floor with their drinks as the dogs gambol among them like ponies. "Oh, Rusty," chides Sally, smiling, as one of the dogs knocks over a drink. She knows that she should introduce Stephen around, but she has already forgotten his name. (And he doesn't help, standing there so defiantly, with his rough red hair.) Involuntarily Sally wonders why Jennifer and Stephen came. Her own three boys are in Jamaica for the holidays with Andrew and Isabel (and their new babies), and she feels a twitch of envy at that thought: the one-upmanship of second marriages. Why didn't she and Alex think of a winter trip?

Alex is still talking about Allison. "The last time I saw her, I was sure she seemed a little better," he says to Jennifer. "Don't you think?"

"I don't know. It's hard to tell." Over the years, she has been as comforting as she can.

Meanwhile, back on Broadway, Allison has waked up. She looks at Maude and then at Jonathan, and then surprisingly she smiles. "Hi, Maude, Jonathan."

"Hi." Softly they ask, "How do you feel?"

"Sleepy. But okay. I think I had too much wine. So many people. I really get confused."

"There were a lot," Maude says.

"But no parents—they're the most confusing—all their names. My father has no idea who he is," says Allison; then asks, "Or were some parents here?" She frowns, in a worried small way. But her eyes have come into focus; they are warm and alert.

Maude tells her, "My mother was here. Louisa. With John. She's married to John Jeffreys now."

"You see?" Allison says. "I get along much better

with doctors. At least they're interchangeable. And my sister—I like Jennifer, and Stephen has the most beautiful hair I ever saw. You have nice hair, too," she says tactfully to Jonathan.

He laughs at her, says, "Thanks."

Allison yawns and stretches, extending arms so thin that all the tiny blue veins show in her wrists. She says, "Maybe I should go to bed."

Maude asks, "You need anything?"

"No, I'm fine. Jennifer showed me where everything was." She faces them both as she stands up, and she says, a little shyly, "You know, I really like it here."

"You can stay," they tell her. "Whenever you want—"

"Okay—" but she is less sure of that. Of staying. She goes over to the staircase, turns and gives them a small wave, and then she goes on up to bed.

She is gone.

Maude tells Jonathan, "That's funny. Just then she looked so well. It's like she slips in and out of being crazy."

"Well, that sort of makes sense, doesn't it? Did she drop a lot of acid, ever?"

"I don't know. I think so." Curiously Maude asks, "Did you?"

"Well, enough. Maybe more than enough. I got scared."

Looking at each other, remembering bad trips, it is suddenly as though their experiences had been simultaneous. Shared. And although they are good friends, having lived for months in the same house, such a large leap toward greater intimacy frightens them both (delicate children), and so they shy back from the edge.

Jonathan says, "How about some music?"

"Great."

He gets up and puts on a record, and the huge room is then suddenly filled with woodwind notes. Flutes and oboes, clarinets.

"Haydn," Jonathan says.

"It's beautiful." Smilingly Maude turns to him. "Jonathan, do you want to do something funny? My mother, Louisa, and John brought a couple of bottles of champagne, and I put them on ice—"

"*Terrific.*"

To anyone who knew them both, it might seem curious that Louisa and Kate, childhood friends from Virginia, now live (both of them) in the Berkeley hills. To them it seems not strange at all but very logical—logical that neither of them has remained in Virginia (who could live in the South?) and that they now live at the farthest edge of the continent, as though pushed there. Southern California would be impossible; why not Berkeley? Lovely views of San Francisco, without that city's danger (yet)—or so the two women see it. And they both find life in Berkeley *interesting:* between themselves they argue voting for the Radical Slate or the April Coalition (they see themselves as closet radicals); they watch meetings on KQED: they patronize the CO-OP. Peace Marches, later on Impeachment Marches. ("Remember the fifties, when we thought poor old Ike was such a terrible President?")

Both women are more politically involved than their husbands are: David says he is too busy, John that he has lost hope.

Their houses, however, are quite dissimilar. Kate's and David's is emphatically modern, with a glassed-in balcony that is cantilevered out from the steep hillside, out into the view. A view of the Bay, of San Francisco and Marin County. Of, tonight, the strangely warm, vividly blue midnight sky.

At the moment Kate is there on the balcony, alone with Jennifer. Kate in a wonderful red silk dress. ("I haven't worn red for years," finding an echoing picture somewhere in her mind.) Kate slimmed down, still a strong and striking woman, intelligent, forthright. And now feeling very confident: she has just got a job, a very good one, as intake social worker in a psychiatric clinic, in Kensington.

This party is to celebrate Kate's job, as well as the onset of the seventies. And Jennifer has brought her remarkable present. It is a blouse, of unbleached muslin—but Jennifer has first pleated the fabric, hundreds of tiny tucks, all beautifully, evenly stitched.

Kate tells her, "Jennifer, it's the most beautiful blouse I ever saw. Really." She is very moved. (So much work!)

"Well, it was fun to make. It must mean I'm crazy or something, but I really dug making all those tucks."

"It's *lovely*."

"And muslin—it should last all your life."

Kate laughs. They have a special understanding of each other, these two women who both appear stronger, less vulnerable than they are; and this is something that each of them knows about the other. Knows and protects.

"Tell me about your job," says Jennifer.

"It's great, but of course I'm sort of ambivalent. It's an institution for rich kids, really. They used to get alcoholics, now they get drugged kids."

"Next year health-food poisoning." Jennifer laughs. Kate, too.

"Well, I know," Kate goes on. "But why aren't I working with black people, in East Oakland? That's more what I had in mind."

"You could work up to Oakland."

Kate would like to tell Jennifer about something that has recently happened to her—something important to her that she has not told anyone else. A man she has known for a long time, now divorced—like David, a successful doctor —that man called her, simply saying that he was in love with her. He was not, he told her, asking her to break up her marriage. ("Not yet," he said; laughed.) But couldn't they—wouldn't she meet him for lunch? Etcetera? (The etcetera unsaid.) Kate had many reactions: she was flattered, pleased, somewhat aroused at the idea of that rangy blond attractive man. And she thought: What restaurant? What motel? San Francisco? Maybe the Palace, lunch first in the Garden Court—she went that far, enjoying plans. And she also thought: What a harmless way to get back at David for that nurse (for possibly quite a few nurses). She ran everything through her mind, and then she listened to her instincts. And she found out that that was not what she wanted to do. For whatever half-understood reasons, she would not. (Instead, that night she and David made love—or, rather, she made love to him—more violently than for years.)

And now she decides not to tell Jennifer. (She is partly thinking of her own mother, Jane Flickinger, who always said too much.)

Kate has gently folded the blouse across her arm; against the red silk sleeve it looks like a delicate pale stole. And delicately Kate touches it. "Jennifer, it's so beautiful," she says again.

Then David comes out to where they are—gray David with a neat gray beard. "Well, I have to keep up with my bearded son," he has said.

"Kate," he now says, "why on earth are we giving a New Year's Eve party? It isn't like us."

"Darling, you know perfectly well why. We decided

to, that's all." She hears her own voice speaking to David, hears her amused affection and the show of strength, and she thinks how little anything changes between people.

"Well, as always, you did a great job, old dear," he says. "Salmon *en croute*—fantastic. And the pâté—like, wow."

"You know I like to show off," she says, observing to herself that he is more careful to praise her than once he might have been. She is not quite sure why: perhaps he sees the emergence (if partial) of a new self of which she herself is not quite aware? (The Kate that their old friend saw?)

She smiles at David; she puts her arm through his. "Christ, almost 1971," she says.

"I know. Whatever will we do with it?"

On the stiff and elaborately carved Victorian sofa where earlier Allison lay uncomfortably asleep, Maude and Jonathan now sit. In front of them is a small table with a pink marble top, which holds their glasses, one empty bottle, and another, almost full.

Maude says, "We look like people posing for something."

They laugh; they have been laughing a lot, off and on, and now they are a little tired.

Jonathan reaches to pour more wine. Then he looks at Maude. With a slightly blurred tone of discovery, he says, "You know, you're really beautiful?"

She looks at him. "Really? I am?"

"Really."

Smiling, he takes her hand; they both have long strong (similar) hands. And then they both face forward again. Fortunately Jonathan is left-handed, and so it is possible to hold hands and sip at drinks at the same time.

"This is a nice high," Maude says.

"Really. And the taste is neat."

"But it's doing something to my nose." Maude laughs, and looks at Jonathan. "Have you ever noticed how much alike we look?" she asks.

"Pale people with long noses," he says, turning to examine her face. "I guess, sort of. But you look much better than I do."

This, too, strikes them as very funny.

Out of a later silence Maude says, "You were really nice with Allison."

"She's nice, I like her a lot."

More quiet minutes pass. (The music has gone off sometime back.) Although Maude and Jonathan are unaware of the time, the new year has arrived.

Then Maude says, "I've got an idea. Why don't we go to bed?"

"Yes." Smiling, he looks at her. They stretch their faces toward each other, they kiss.

Jonathan asks, "But which bed, yours or mine?"

They laugh, both of them shy and a little nervous. Maude says, "I think my room's more private."

Gathering their glasses and the bottle, they go upstairs to bed.